"You said that we must talk, Karim."

"Yes." He spread his hands in a fatalistic gesture. "That is all we have left between us—talk."

Linda stood there silently and disbelieved him. Whatever his conscience drove him to believe, she knew that those clenched hands of his were longing to glide over her skin—and that her skin was yearning for their touch.

A sigh escaped her as his eyes focused on her shapeliness through the sheer, clinging robe.

"You had better get dressed," he said curtly, turning away. "I would like you to put on something less provocative."

"How can I provoke you, Karim, when there is nothing left between us?"

"Damn you scowling
to strike
Then he
her close
descend

Books by Violet Winspear

HARLEQUIN PRESENTS

HARLEQUIN ROMANCE

These books may be available at your local bookseller.

Don't miss any of our special offers. Write to us at the following address for information on our newest releases.

Harlequin Reader Service
P.O. Box 52040, Phoenix, AZ 85072-2040
Canadian address: P.O. Box 2800, Postal Station A,
5170 Yonge St., Willowdale, Ont. M2N 6J3

VIOLET WINSPEAR

sun lord's woman

Harlequin Books

TORONTO • NEW YORK • LONDON
AMSTERDAM • PARIS • SYDNEY • HAMBURG
STOCKHOLM • ATHENS • TOKYO • MILAN

"It is in the half-light of the Bedouin Arab tent
that one must seek the model of true love."

Stendhal

Harlequin Presents first edition January 1986
ISBN 0-373-10854-0

Original hardcover edition published in 1985
by Mills & Boon Limited

CHAPTER ONE

GREY-green agave lined the undulating road and there were silver-green terraces of olive trees and bright oleanders. The road curved round and round, heading towards the rocky plateau where her destination lay.

Dust rose in a cloud behind the wheels of the cab and a sheer drop to the sea lay on the left side of the vehicle. White stone houses hung on the hillside and the occasional figure in black shielded dark eyes with a hand and watched the cab go speeding by in its web of dust, so that within seconds those figures vanished out of sight like apparitions.

Everything had a dreamlike quality for Linda who was still feeling slightly strange after being high in the air and then almost too soon down on the ground again. She had enjoyed her first flight but had been glad to escape the noise and confusion of the airport when the great jet touched down. Thanks to those many evenings of Spanish lessons she had been able to get through the routine of landing without any difficulty and when she had stepped out of the terminal into the brilliant sunlight she had simply joined the queue and waited her turn for a cab.

Now she could relax and enjoy the scenery through which she was being driven along the coastal road way above the *Bahia Conchas* which, translated, meant the Bay of Shells. The sea was a rippling, dazzling blue and the air that rushed in through the open window beside her was laden with the scents of this wonderfully strange land, old in history, warm and passionate, yet with an underlying strain of barbarity.

Not only was this the land of the brilliant oleander and the velvety red geranium that could reach to the very roof of a white house, it was where blood was spilled on the sand of the bullring, and the shadow of the Secret Court of the Holy Cross still lay over the culture of its people. The penitents still walked through the streets on holy days and lashed themselves with knotted ropes.

Land of whitegold sun and black shadows intermingling. Of sensuality and a sombre sadness in its music and in the dark eyes that studied a foreign woman so curiously.

Linda felt exhilarated by all she saw and felt, for though it had been a wrench to leave her aunt and uncle, she had so longed to come here. Few people suspected that her cool, self-contained manner concealed a nature which had longed for the brazen sun beating down on this bold land of bulls, the flamenco and the language of the fan. Here in the south, time had stood still and only the infrequent car on the coastal road brought a glimpse of city life to the people working their fields and vines.

And each spin of the wheel carried Linda a little nearer to another meeting with Don Ramos who in every way had seemed to typify the handsome, volatile Latin. She had looked into his eyes and seen a man who probably took the admiration of women as his due.

He had probably summed her up as an impressionable country girl, and she couldn't help wishing that she was more worldly. She wondered what it would feel like to be the object of ardent attention from Don Ramos Gil de Torres. When she briefly closed her eyes she seemed to see his darkly handsome face again, and the beige suit like a second skin covering his agile looking frame. And if she concentrated really hard she seemed to feel the warm touch of his hand.

Her heart gave a crazy little lurch when she recalled the moment when he briefly touched her upon returning her handbag to her lap. It was then she had noticed the ring of heavy plaited gold on one of his fingers.

A little sigh crept from her lips. Whether married or single Don Ramos was as far out of her reach as the Spanish Sierras, but there was nothing to stop her from romancing about him, just as she sometimes did when she sat in the velvety dimness of a cinema and watched a favourite actor. The cinema, so she had read, had its foundations in the dreams of lonely people and she supposed there was a certain truth in the belief.

Better to love the unattainable than not to love at all, and a screen idol could never break your heart as a living person could. He remained for always the ideal hero whom familiarity could never turn into a fallible human being whose ways might be less perfect than his face and form. Though his arms could never hold you, his eyes looked out from the screen and a subtle form of communication took place.

It was magnetism and Linda had felt the pull of it ever since starting the drive along this coast road to *La Granja Vista*. Her heart beat fast with anticipation; she longed for her first sight of the house and felt sure it would live up to her every expectation and have something of a Moorish look about it.

Suddenly the driver of the cab flung some words over his shoulder and even as Linda caught his meaning the cab lurched into an object on the road and spun out of control. The motion hurled Linda head first against the seat in front, she felt a stunning pain as her brow struck the edge of the seat and then had a sensation of falling backwards into a black void.

She lay unconscious and unaware on the back seat of the cab whose rear wheels spun in the air above a sheer drop to the ocean which creamed and tumbled over the boulders jutting below the cliffside. The obstacle which the cab had struck lay there in the centre of the road, a large sack of vegetables which had fallen unnoticed from a farmer's truck.

Linda's life hung in the balance while the cab driver prayed to every holy saint he could think of. But for his considerable bulk and his foot jammed down hard on the brake they couldn't have hung on, and even when a large car rounded the bend with two men inside the cab driver continued to beseech the saints to preserve him for the sake of his wife, his four children, his mother and an assortment of aunts, uncles and cousins.

With the utmost speed the cab was roped to the back axle of the limousine whose engine was kept running by the chauffeur while the owner gave the cab driver the order to leap clear the instant he had hold of the girl.

A terrific crash combined with the sting of cognac on her tongue brought Linda to her senses. She choked as the fiery liquid ran down her throat, and weakly she tried to push the flask from her lips.

'A little more.' There was something about the voice that made her submit, and when her eyes fluttered open she found herself gazing up dazedly at a very brown, intensely strong face, the eyes flickering behind the narrowed eyelids of a man who lived perpetually in the sun. She had the strangest feeling that she knew him but her head was pounding so painfully that she couldn't think of his name, or how she came to be in his arms on the wide and comfortable back seat of a sumptuous car that seemed to be travelling in space.

'You have taken a nasty knock, *señorita*. When we arrive at the *castillo* you must be put to bed.'

Bed! Linda struggled against the pain and confusion in her head. 'W-why am I here?'

'You will remember in a while,' he assured her, and he extended the cognac flask to someone who sat in the front part of the big car. 'Take some of this, *amigo*. You, too, have suffered a nasty shock.'

'*Si, señor*, but for the intervention of your sainted self the *Inglesa* and myself would have crashed into the sea with my poor vehicle.'

'You are insured, I hope?' Linda heard the deep timbre of the voice above her head and again she had a feeling of familiarity.

Whatever had happened? She strove to remember . . . fragments of a broken picture shifted about in her head and then very slowly they began to fit together. 'The cab—it crashed into something!' she exclaimed.

'So now it all begins to come back to you, eh?'

She searched the dark, strong face above hers and that odd sense of familiarity began to recede. No, she had never seen or met this man before—who on earth could he be?

And as if he read her thoughts he supplied the answer. 'I am Karim el Khalid de Torres,' he informed her. 'And do you recall your own name, *señorita*?'

'Yes, I'm Linda Layne.' She gazed at him almost incredulously, for the man who had interviewed her at the Royale Hotel had been named Don Ramos Gil de

Torres. The two were somehow related and that was why she had seen shadings of that other Spanish face in the features of this man.

'I—I'm on my way to *La Granja Vista*,' she said, making an attempt to withdraw herself from this dark stranger's arms . . . and, mercy, what muscular arms they were, like bonds of leather around her.

'You are feeling a little stronger?' he asked.

She nodded. 'W-what happened to the cab?'

'It went over the cliffside and you almost went with it. My driver and I came along and we were able to be of assistance.'

Linda shuddered as she recalled the sound of the cab falling with a resounding crash over the cliffside.

'Then you saved our lives, *señor?*'

'I expect we did.'

'Thank you.'

'A legend of my father's country says that if a man saves a life or two he obtains keys into the innermost regions of Paradise.'

It was impossible for Linda to tell if he was amused by the legend or not, for his half-lowered eyelids made his gaze as inscrutable as she had heard it said of Eastern eyes. As she again made an effort to draw away from him, he relaxed his hold and she was able to shift her proximity to him.

She allowed her head to rest against the soft leather of the car seat and when the pounding quietened a little she voiced the question which had been clamouring for an answer ever since he had told her his name.

'Are you related to Señora Valcarel Novalis?'

'We are cousins,' he replied. 'And you, I realise, go to *La Granja Vista* to be the *compañera* of her daughter. Is this not so, Señorita Layne?'

'Yes—it was fortunate you were travelling the same road, *señor*.'

'Was it fortune or was it fate?' he murmured.

In view of his obvious mixed parentage Linda decided that he would take the latter word to be the most fitting. Kismet, as the Arabs termed it. 'Are you on your way to visit the *señora*, your cousin?' she asked.

'Not exactly.' A dry note of humour had entered his voice. 'It would seem that you are unaware of the layout of the *granja*.'

'Yes,' she admitted, and wondered what other surprise fate held in store for her today.

'The *granja*,' he explained, 'is a property on my land in which Dona Domaya lives with her child. When she became widowed in the appalling uprisings that swept Latin America, where her husband Luis a much-respected physician was taken with many others and never seen again, I did for her in some respects what I did for you a short while ago, I pulled her out of a situation of risk and she came to live on my estate. You, *señorita*, will be living on my estate, the British companion who, I understand, will be teaching music to Pepita as well as English.'

'Yes, *señor*.' She sat absorbing his words, for during her interview with Don Ramos she had been told none of this. There had been no indication that Pepita and her mother had been rescued from a terrible situation ... and Linda realised from newspaper accounts what shocking things had occurred during the military coups which had taken place in certain Latin countries.

With her head still aching and in a whirl, Linda closed her eyes and let her thoughts drift back to her meeting with Don Ramos Gil de Torres. The evening

before the interview in London she had made it plain
to Aunt Doris that she meant to accept the job if she
proved to be a suitable applicant. Always there had
been opposition to any plans she made for herself, and
this time she firmly told her aunt that at the age of
twenty-three she was entitled to go abroad if she
wished. She didn't want to marry Larry Nevins, the
son of a family friend; she yearned to see something of
the world and Spain had always beckoned her.

Of course, there had been the usual recriminations.
Linda had been reminded of all her aunt and uncle
had done for her since at the age of ten she had
been sent to live with them following the breakdown
of her parents' marriage. And on her side there had
been the usual repetition of how grateful she would
always be for her upbringing and her education
which because of her uncle's great interest in music
had resulted in her own scholarship to the London
College of Music.

Linda had loved being a student there but the fact
remained that she didn't wish to take up the offer to
join what she admitted was a renowned orchestra. Her
secret dream had been to achieve the perfection of a
soloist but as it turned out she missed by a hair's
breadth that perfect control over the cello. Professor
Lindiscarne told her again and again that she was
more highly strung than the instrument and it had to
be the other way around; she had to be in absolute
control of the cello, a very temperamental instrument
for all its size.

So she had refused the orchestral offer and replied
instead to an advertisement which she had actually
come across in *The Lady*, a magazine her aunt
subscribed to. She had written to the box number
stated in the advertisement and a few days later

received a reply from a London hotel requesting that she attend for an interview the next Friday—which happened to be a Friday the thirteenth.

'I hope it turns out unlucky for you,' Aunt Doris said, a woman always torn between bursts of affection and a sudden, quite appalling bitchiness. Linda had endured this seesaw life for thirteen years and when she held in her hand the letter from Señora Valcarel Novalis she prayed that she would achieve this chance to go and work in Spain.

When Friday came and the cab set her down in front of the Royale Hotel in Mayfair she braced her spine as she went towards the swing-doors where a doorman in a beige and brown uniform gave her a look that took her in from her ankles to her light gold hair fringed above eyes of an almost startlingly, clear honey colour. Beneath those eyes her nose had a slight tilt to it, and beneath her nose her mouth was wide and generous.

Linda entered the foyer where the carpet felt ankle deep, and she tried to look as if she walked into hotels in Mayfair every day of her life. The clerk behind the imposing desk eyed the suburban style of her suit and seemed to know better.

'I've an appointment with Señora Valcarel Novalis,' she informed him. 'My name is Linda Layne and I'm to see her at three o'clock.'

The rather effete young man checked with the clock on the wall of the reception area, then he picked up the telephone and requested a room number of the switchboard operator. As he spoke Linda's name into the mouthpiece he continued to look at her with an air of superiority.

'Miss Layne?' He arched an eyebrow which she could have sworn was plucked. 'Will you please wait in reception and someone will arrive shortly to confer with you.'

'Thank you.' She moved away from the desk and sat down in one of the deep couches placed within reach of low tables with smoked-glass surfaces. Her legs felt trembly, just as if she were about to play a piece of music for the examiners at the college. She had arrived right on time and had expected to be interviewed almost at once, but when she again glanced at the clock it was twenty minutes past three and she began to wonder if the *señora* had decided on someone else for the job.

Linda's heart sank. She had painted bright pictures of Spain in her mind and now they were fading and losing their colour. It had been stupid of her to imagine that she was the only applicant ... and there her thoughts broke off as she noticed a very assured looking man approaching the reception desk where he paused to speak to the clerk, who gestured in her direction.

The man was noticeable in every way and Linda found her eyes fixed upon him as he came towards the couch where she sat. He wore a superbly cut suit which fitted him like a glove, showing every supple line of his body. He looked and walked like a matador minus the cloak and when he paused in front of Linda she felt stunned by his good looks.

'You are Señorita Layne?'

'Y-yes.' She felt she ought to stand up but the depths of the couch were holding her like a quicksand and when she made the attempt her handbag slid from her lap and she felt overwhelmingly gauche as he bent and picked it up for her.

'Don't be nervous.' He spoke English but it was overlaid by his Latin accent, and as he returned her bag to her lap he sat down beside her. 'My sister is indisposed so I came to conduct the interview in her place. I am Don Ramos Gil de Torres and you are the young Englishwoman from Essex who wrote Domaya such a very sensible letter.'

Something in the way he spoke the word, some indefinable thread of mockery, instantly warned Linda that she must pull herself together. She had written a sensible letter but her gaucherie implied that she was lacking in the composure required by a Spanish family when it came to choosing a companion.

'You state in your letter, Señorita Layne, that you have no previous experience of being a *compañera*—why would you suddenly wish to take up such an occupation?'

How deep his voice, how seductive and yet still a trifle mocking. Linda felt compelled to look at him and found his sensuous gaze on her lips.

'The idea strikes me as interesting,' she replied. 'I would like to give it a try.'

'Then allow me to inform you, *señorita*, that my sister was very impressed by your letter and I was told that if you matched its sensibility I was to offer you the position.'

Linda controlled her rising sense of excitement and regarded him with a look of gravity. 'What have you decided, *señor*?'

'You speak well,' he replied. 'You dress neatly and your hair and fingernails are speckless—what more could any doting mother want in a companion for her daughter?'

'Are you saying that I'm hired, *señor*?' Linda felt a fluttering inside her as if her heart grew a pair of wings.

'By all means consider yourself hired, *señorita*.'

'And can you tell me when I start my job?'

'I shall give you all the details over coffee and cakes.' He rose to his feet and extended a hand in order to assist her from the couch. 'Come, we shall go into the lounge where in a very few minutes they will start to serve afternoon refreshments.'

An hour later Linda emerged from the Royale Hotel in a daze of delight. And as her train sped through Essex the wheels seemed to hammer out the refrain: 'Linda Layne, you are going to Spain ... going to Spain ... to Spain.'

And there in Spain she would see Don Ramos again, for in every way he had imprinted himself upon her mind. He was a man, she secretly thought, who could hurt a woman and yet make of it a memory worth every ounce of heartache.

She stirred out of her thoughts and as her eyes opened, her gaze locked with that of the man who just a short while ago had saved her life. His gaze was intent and now she had regained her senses she saw how very much of an Arab he was, with heavy brows shading the slope of very dark eyes, his detailed cheekbones stabbed by sideburns on a level with the bold outline of his lips. He emitted an air of ruthless authority which the modern cut of his suit did nothing to tone down. His resemblance to the handsome Don Ramos was lost in the brooding set of his features as he contemplated her slim figure, languid and still slightly in shock there against the yielding leather of the seat they shared.

'You appear very young to be a companion,' he said abruptly. '*Compañeras* in the household when I was a boy were dumpy women on the wrong side of forty, either fussing or put upon. Times change, eh?'

'Yes,' she agreed, feeling uncertain about a man who

made her think of black tents low against the burning sand of the desert. She thought he should be wearing a cloak that wrapped him from neck to booted heel, and realised that in just a matter of hours she had travelled from the pastoral green fields of home into a land where mysticism went hand in hand with cruelty; where a man's courtesy could disguise an attitude towards women that was one of master and slave.

Instinctively she wanted to draw as far away from this man as she possibly could. Although he had saved her life, she saw something in his eyes that was almost speculative, as if he might be thinking that she owed him a favour in return for what he had done.

Her gaze fell to his shoulders, then to his hands which even in repose had a dark look of power in keeping with his face and form. He glanced at the golden face of his watch on a dark leather strap that contrasted with the crisp white cuff of his shirt. 'In just a few minutes, *señorita*, we reach the gates of the *castillo*. I take into account the shock of your experience but I have the feeling my cousin Ramos skated over certain details and left you to imagine a cosier domain than the one you now approach.'

Abruptly he leaned close to Linda and she breathed a strong fragrant tobacco and a whiff of equally strong soap. Though dark, his skin was burnished and she saw the white edge of his teeth against the bold curve of his mouth.

'He never for a moment mentioned me, did he?'

Her heart seemed to thud against her breastbone and she could feel herself straining back against the leather upholstery. She shook her head which hurt and swam at the motion. Pain must have registered on her face for his gaze lifted to her brow which was mottled by a bruise. 'Your welcome to Spain has been one of mixed blessings, eh? I hope that neither I nor the misfortune to the cab has made you have regrets about coming here?'

'No,' she said, 'even though I've lost my luggage.'

'Ah, now that is a catastrophe in a woman's eyes!' Something gleamed in his eyes, like a tiny comet falling through their density. 'You are thinking to yourself that you are in the depths of Spain so where on earth will you acquire a toothbrush, a lipstick and a change of clothing. Correct?'

'Yes.' She was distressed by an image of her belongings scattered in the wreckage of the cab. She had spent savings on light and supple dresses suitable for a southern climate, and now they were ruined before she even had a chance to wear them. Tears brimmed in her eyes, for it seemed as if her aunt's prediction that she was making the biggest mistake of her life was starting to come true.

'You mark my words,' Aunt Doris had said, 'you'll come running home to us from that land of barbarians! They're no better than the Romans who used to watch the Christians being torn limb from limb by lions!'

'Tears?' A hard thumb grazed her skin as Karim el Khalid wiped a teardrop from her cheek. 'I should not have taken you for a young woman who puts all her stock in possessions.'

The feel of him touching her face didn't thrill her in the same way Don Ramos had thrilled her. This was a totally different feeling . . . there was fear in it.

'I—I haven't so many possessions that I can afford to lose them,' she rejoined. 'You live in a castle and drive about in a sumptuous car so you wouldn't understand what it means to spend most of your savings on clothes suitable for your new job only to have them ruined. I don't suppose you have any idea what it's like to depend on a salary—I expect the suit you're wearing cost more than all the things I've lost!'

'I expect you are right in your assumption, Señorita Layne.' He leaned away from her and his shaded mouth and jaw seemed to her to have a touch of cruelty about them. 'Your wardrobe will be replaced, I assure you. Dona Domaya will probably take a trip to San Lopez in the near future, but in the meantime you need not feel bereft of any essentials. When the military coups in Latin America were at their height my home was a refuge for those in flight, people who had nothing with them but their battered lives. Clothing of all kinds was kept in stock at the *castillo* so I feel sure Adoracion will be able to supply you with most of what you need.'

'Thank you, *señor*.' Linda had reached the point of an almost numb acceptance of this man's ability to take charge. She had a vision of being kitted out in a hodge-podge of clothing, and idly wondered who Adoracion was. It was one of those beautiful Spanish names derived from their religion so the woman was probably his wife.

Behind the shield of her lashes Linda studied his profile ... to look at he seemed more Arab than Spanish so he probably took after his father though he chose to live in Spain. Rich as the devil, no doubt, who in the way of the feudal lord of the locality had thrown open his castle doors to those who had escaped the reign of terror which the military had let loose in countries such as Chile and Argentina.

He looked, she thought, like a man who enjoyed danger and Linda realised that risk had been involved when he had snatched her from the back seat of a vehicle which was on the verge of plunging down the cliffs into the sea. The thought of what she had escaped made her toes curl inside her shoes, but a maddening little voice whispered in her mind that she was beholden to Karim el Khalid and he looked as if he collected his debts even if he could be generous with his courage and his castle.

He was unlike any other man she had ever met in her life; there were alien forces in his face, and the very sands of the desert seemed to grate in his throat when he spoke to her.

'We arrive at the *castillo*.' He gestured with a sunburned hand as the big car swept between towering iron gates into a tremendous forecourt where a fountain held a shimmering image of the castle in its archway of sunlit water.

CHAPTER TWO

THE castle against the sky was the most romantic silhouette Linda had ever seen and she gazed in fascination at the contrast in height of the roofs and turrets.

It was a wonderfully evocative skyline in honey-coloured stone, the curving walls of the barbican as beautiful as they were powerful, the arched bridge having been made for horsemen rather than a limousine.

She could hardly believe in the reality of the place, yet there it stood and the man who assisted her from the car was its lord and master. It wasn't until she stepped from the car and stood in front of Karim el Khalid that she realised how tall he was, his shoulders seeming to strain at the dark suit jacket that covered them. 'Come!' He gripped her by the elbow and she mounted the wide flank of steps beside him, to where the great arch of a door stood open into a high-roofed hall rich with panelling, stained glass and massive furniture.

The place and the man suddenly overpowered Linda and she felt her legs giving way beneath her. Even as she sagged a pair of strong arms caught hold of her and she was lifted into them as easily as if she had been a child.

Oh Lord, she thought weakly. What a way to begin her job. She had come to take care of a child and instead was being carried into one of the *castillo* rooms because she needed some care and attention herself.

23

'I—I'm sorry to be such a bother,' she said weakly.

'You have been admirably controlled.' El Khalid lowered her into the velvet arms of a high-backed chair. 'Many would have been in quite a state after such an experience. Lean back your head, *señorita*. Rest and recover while I ring for coffee and have a bedroom prepared for you.'

'But I——' Linda gazed at him with a trapped look in her eyes. 'I can't stay here! Dona Domaya expects me at her house!'

'I shall send a message to Dona Domaya explaining what has happened.' He strode across the room to where a push-button was set in the wall beside an arching fireplace made from slabs of stone. Linda hadn't expected to see fireplaces in a Spanish house but she realised that in the wintertime it would be cold this high above the sea. She watched helplessly as her host prodded the bell with his finger, then with an almost silken control of his body he turned to confront her.

'A cup of coffee will help to restore you, but I am wondering if a doctor should take a look at you. My driver could fetch the *medico* from the village in half an hour——'

'No,' Linda shook her head, 'the dizziness has passed a-and I truly feel all right apart from a headache. Can't your driver take me to Dona Domaya's house? It would save you the bother of having me here.'

'Do I appear to be bothered, *señorita*?' He stood tall against the arching fireplace, the thumbs of his hands resting in the pockets of the waistcoat that was matt-black in contrast to the pin-striping of his suit. 'The responsibility of a single young Englishwoman isn't likely to thread my hair with grey.'

A remark which drew her gaze to his hair which was thick and black above his observant eyes. For a brief, heart-racing moment Linda stared into the unfathomable darkness of his eyes and saw in them a look of mastery that made her want to take to her heels and run.

If only Don Ramos would walk in and take charge of her ... instead a maid in a discreet uniform entered and was given the order to fetch coffee to the *sala*.

'*Si, patron.*' A swift look was cast in Linda's direction as the woman withdrew, and Linda was left with the distinct impression that when the *patron* gave orders in his deep and vigorous voice those around him lost no time carrying them out.

'I am aware that the British are addicted to their cup of tea,' he remarked, 'but you will enjoy our coffee, and in due course I hope you will enjoy Spain. Is this the first time you have travelled to a foreign land?'

'Yes, *señor*.'

'You had the sudden wish to spread your wings, eh?'

Linda nodded and thought of past tussles with Aunt Doris whenever she had voiced this wish to travel beyond the limits of her aunt's suburban world, neatly encompassed by the privet hedge of the mock-Tudor house with the coach-lamp hanging in the porch. A house that was a twin to every other dwelling in the quiet, self-contained neighbourhood where the offspring learned to ride and play tennis at the Kingswood Country Club and intermarried with each other.

A pattern of life which Linda could no longer endure once she left college, especially when she felt pressure being put upon her to become engaged to Larry Nevins. Lanky Larry as he was called at the club, a young man who paled into total insignificance the day Don Ramos walked into her life.

From that moment Linda had felt that her fate was sealed, that she had to go to Spain and dismiss the hurtful words flung at her by Aunt Doris the evening before her departure. Accusations that she was no better than her selfish, runaway mother who would regret ever setting foot on foreign soil where she would be at the mercy of a lot of strangers whose ways were entirely different from those of English people.

'That, *señorita*, was a very deep sigh.' The voice broke in upon her thoughts. 'Are you thinking that your first few hours in Spain have been traumatic ones?'

'Yes,' she admitted. 'My relatives didn't want me to take work in Spain—they were very opposed to it.'

'Because you are quite young, eh?'

'I'm twenty-three, *señor*.'

'Ah, what a very advanced age,' he mocked. 'Wait until you are thirty-six when no doubt you will feel very ancient.'

'Of course not,' she said, and secretly thought to herself that El Khalid looked every year of his age, as if responsibility combined with the hot sun had etched those lines that framed his features. He wasn't just a man with a tan; she could see that his skin was naturally that deep shade of brown and she could feel herself following his movements as he sat down in a large chair of cardinal-red leather. On the wall beyond his chair there was an immense El Greco storm painting which seemed to blend in with El Khalid's air of authority. An authority which boded trouble for anyone who opposed him when he believed himself to be in the right.

She felt the strangest of thoughts as she watched

him, a man tinged by a certain dark and distant loneliness. He could have been one of those monks of the *auto da fe* which she had read about when Spain began to take a grip on her imagination. Or perhaps a sorcerer who cast spells in this castle which was so remote from a suburban existence with its routines and its conventional attitudes.

'It was the way you spoke,' she said, breaking into speech because his silence unnerved her, 'as if you thought me a teenager.'

'My humble apologies.' His lips curled amusedly. 'I tend to forget how easy it is to prick young skin which has not had time to harden.'

As his eyes flicked her skin Linda put a hand to the base of her throat where the beat of her heart could be felt beneath her fingertips. She felt a stab of intense relief when the door opened and the maid carried a silver tray to an oval table whose carved woodwork had a deep-red gleam to it. Linda could see that the coffee set was of old and lustrous silver and the instant the coffee was poured into the cups of fluted bone-china the aroma filled her with longing. She took brown sugar and just a dash of cream in her cup and was aware of El Khalid speaking in his grating Spanish to the maid as she enjoyed the best cup of coffee she had ever tasted.

'*Muy fino, señorita?*'

His voice broke in on her sense of enjoyment and she ventured a Spanish word in response. '*Vaya, señor.*'

He quirked an eyebrow. 'You speak a little Spanish?'

'I've been taking lessons,' she admitted. 'I'm not too sure of my pronunciation but I hope to improve on that.'

'So you are quite determined to be the thoroughly efficient *compañera*.' He strolled across with the coffee pot and refilled her cup. 'Did you understand anything of what I said to the *servidora*?'

'Yes, I think you mentioned my *permiso de residencia*.'

'Quite so.' He hoisted a well-clad foot upon a leather footstool near Linda's chair. 'When I retrieved you from the cab there was no time to save your handbag and I guess that your permit to reside, with your work visa and passport were in the bag. It may be possible to recover them and I have given orders that some men go at once to search the wreckage. The rest of your luggage was in the boot, eh?'

She nodded and gave him a hopeful look. 'Do you think——?'

'I am not too optimistic as the cab plunged from the cliffs in a backward motion but your handbag was with you in the interior and it may have survived. We must hope so. Spanish law isn't too flexible about these matters and if the permit and visa are irrecoverable then applications will have to be made again.'

Linda's look turned to one of anxiety. 'Do you mean that I shan't be allowed to stay if my papers can't be found?'

'You will not be allowed to work, so instead you will stay as my guest.'

'But I——'

'You are a little too fond of arguing with a man.' Although he spoke jestingly there was a look in his eyes which warned Linda that he wasn't in the habit of being opposed by any woman. 'Surely it would be of interest to you to be a guest in a Spanish castle?'

'You don't seem to understand——' Agitation was

making her head ache again. 'I have no money, *señor*. I need to work so I can be paid my wages!'

'Ah, so it's the thought of *pesetas* which puts that look of alarm in your eyes. You see yourself as a penniless person in my house, eh? Your sense of pride is affronted by the idea?'

'Can you wonder at it?' She felt close to tears again and had to fight against them . . . a few hours ago she had stepped from the great aircraft with such high hopes and now she was in the house of a stranger and all she had in the world were the clothes on her back.

'Let me point something out to you, *señorita*.' He stood to his full height, making her feel more than ever in his power. 'I snatched you from the brink of death and that imposes upon you the obligation of accepting my hospitality. A graceful acceptance would be more to my liking but you are obviously an independent female who reacts against male authority. Even at this moment I know that if you could summon the strength you would dash from my house.'

He shook his head at her as if quizzically intrigued by a penniless female who dared to show him pride and resistance.

'I—I barely know you,' she breathed. 'You could easily arrange for me to be taken to Dona Domeya's house but you—you insist that I stay here.'

'I do insist.' He snapped back the lid of a carved humidor and took from it a leaf-wrapped cigar which crackled in his fingers. 'Do you mind if I smoke, *señorita*?'

'It's your house,' she rejoined.

His eyes fixed themselves upon her pale but defiant face. 'I told you, did I not, that Dona Domaya and her daughter were brought to Spain in painful circumstances. She has not yet recovered from the experience and, quite frankly, is not the best of persons to have charge of a young woman in your present state of shock and confusion. Tomorrow all may be well.'

He paused and took his time lighting his cigar; as the air filled with its aroma he paced about the room, across the beautifully tiled floor where soft rugs were scattered. Above his head was a ceiling of carved wood from which hung a set of Moorish lamps. There were cabinets of honey-coloured wood heavily inlaid with silver and pearl, and inside them Linda could see antique books and ornaments.

'Tomorrow,' he resumed, 'you may be in possession of your papers and therefore free to do as you wish. But in the event that your handbag and its contents are beyond recovery, then you will stay here at the *castillo* as my guest.'

It was the positive way he spoke the words that made Linda sit up and react with defiance. 'I don't see the need——'

'I do.' He cut straight across her statement. 'At the present time my cousin Ramos is sharing the *granja* with his sister and there is a certain protocol attached to these matters. You are now in Spain, remember.'

'How could I possibly forget?' Linda pressed a hand to her brow and wondered why she defied this arrogant man when it was so much easier to let him have his way. 'I—I don't quite understand your reasoning, *señor*. What difference does it make if Don Ramos is staying with his sister? In the event that my papers are recovered, then I shall be working and living at the *granja*.'

'As a respectable *compañera*.'

Linda stared at El Khalid through the smoke that wreathed his dark head and realised with a jolt what he was inferring. A single girl in Spain had to be careful

of her reputation, and if it became necessary for her to
reapply for a permit to work and reside, the authorities
might refuse her application if they felt dubious about
her.

'Why does it make a difference if I stay under your
roof?' she asked. 'Is it because you are a married man
and Don Ramos is a bachelor?'

Smoke slid from his lips in a deliberate way. 'It is
because I hold a position of authority, *señorita*, and
because Ramos is the married man—albeit one who
lives apart from his wife.'

Linda absorbed in silence the painful impact of his
words . . . it was something she had suspected but to
have it confirmed seemed to seal her doom, as it were.
She either accepted El Khalid's offer of hospitality or
she asked him to buy her a return ticket to England
where her aunt would insist that she put out of her
mind now and for always the idea of working for
foreigners.

In the silence that hung on the air with the rich blue
smoke, a silence strangely unbroken by the revolving
ceiling fans at either end of the room, Linda formed a
mental picture of her aunt's face if she were ever to see
Karim el Khalid de Torres, who looked as if he could
wipe off the tennis court every member of the
Kingswood Country Club.

'Very well,' she said, her voice husky with nerves,
'I'll do as you say.'

He went at once to the bell on the wall and stabbed
it with his finger. 'You look exhausted and by now
Adoracion will have had a room prepared for you. I
recommend that you sleep until this evening when you
may feel like coming downstairs for dinner. We dine
quite late, when the cool of the evening sets in.'

For now, Linda thought wearily, she would allow

him to order her life, but she would hope and pray that his searchers found her handbag and made it possible for her to take up her role of companion to Dona Domaya's daughter. He seemed to her to be splitting hairs over this matter of Spanish protocol, for in every way Linda felt him to be far more dangerous to a woman's reputation than the charming Latin whom she had met at the Royale Hotel.

Not for a moment had Don Ramos made her feel as she felt right now, as if a dark hawk had swooped upon her and held her struggling in his talons.

She gave a little gasp and came back to herself to find El Khalid leaning over her with his hands upon her shoulders. 'Come, you are falling off to sleep. Adoracion will lead the way to your room.' And even as she braced herself against his touch he swung her up into his arms, making her catch her breath at the thought of so much easy strength . . . so much masculine power.

As he strode with her to the door she saw the woman who stood there, dark hair drawn back severely from an unsmiling face, her hands clasped against the dark material of her dress. She showed no reaction at all to the sight of the *patron* carrying towards a huge flight of stairs a young woman who was so obviously English.

Linda felt the oddest mixture of sensations as she was carried up those kingly stairs that branched into a gallery lit by a large round window rich with colour. The stately woman in black indicated the mahogany double-doors of a room about halfway along the gallery, and the *patron* paused while the doors were opened, and he firmly carried Linda into a high, wide and handsome bedroom fit for a princess rather than someone who had come to Spain with the intention of being a companion.

As he slid her to her feet Linda tried to be unaware that the curves of her body had brushed the hardness of his chest. She felt his eyes on her face, and then he turned to Adoracion. 'You were able to find suitable bed attire for the *señorita*?' and he spoke in English as if to inform Linda that she would have no difficulty communicating with the woman who had such a beguiling name and yet who looked so unemotional.

Adoracion indicated the garments laid upon the gorgeously patterned throwover which had a lavish fringe that reached to the carpet. He moved to the bedside and picked up the nightdress and its matching wrap, and Linda watched in a kind of fascinated fear as he slid one of his strong dark hands beneath the filmy fabric, as if he might be visualising the shape of her beneath the apricot translucence.

'It is like something out of a harem,' he mused.

'I was told nightwear for a young woman,' Adoracion replied. 'I can find replacements if the *patron* is displeased.'

'I am wondering if the *señorita* is displeased?' He looked directly at Linda who assumed what she hoped was a look of disinterest.

'I'm grateful that you found something for me to wear.'

'You are rocking on your feet.' He replaced the nightdress on the bed. 'After you have rested you will feel better about things, and if when you awake you feel like dining downstairs, then please inform Adoracion and she will find you a suitable dress.'

He crossed the room to the twin doors where he gave her a polite and imperturbable bow. 'Sleep and mend,' he said, and the doors closed almost silently behind his departure.

Linda wished that Adoracion had followed the

patron, but instead she stood there in a chilling silence, as if resentful of the fact that she had been given orders to wait on a mere *compañera.* In a mood of quiet desperation Linda glanced around the room; were all the rooms in the castle as grand as this one? She felt quite convinced from the Spanish woman's manner that she would have been given an attic to sleep in if Adoracion could have got away with it. No doubt she ruled the staff with a rod of iron but in her turn she was overruled by El Khalid.

Linda's gaze took in the sheer net ready to be draped around the bed and attached to a decorative coronet high against the painted ceiling. The throw-over was all the colours in a peacock's tail and never in her life had she seen so enormous a wardrobe, inset with a long oval mirror carved around the rim with imps and satyrs. Sunlight was made into patterns by the filigreed ironwork of the window grilles, and the warmth seemed to intensify the scent of dried bay leaves that hung in the air.

The sunlight sent a dart of pain to Linda's brow and she stroked her fingers across her forehead. She wasn't asking for sympathy but the gesture seemed to have an effect on Adoracion.

'I will fetch *agua de colonia* for the headache,' she said, and the black fabric of her dress made a rustling sound as she left the room. A sound, Linda thought, as if she walked through dry, fallen leaves.

Linda waited a few moments, then she approached the doors and glanced outside, wondering which door along the gallery gave access to the bathroom. As tired as she felt she wanted to take a shower, feeling certain that it would ease her aching head far more than the rather sickly tang of cologne water.

She decided to risk an investigation and crossed

beneath the rainbow glow of the big round window and tried one of the single doors. The handle turned and a glance inside revealed shelves of neatly arranged bed linen and blankets, and she breathed again that tang of bay leaves. At the next turn of a handle she was relieved to find herself in a large bathroom tiled not in white but in the pale emerald-green of the sea above which the *castillo* was lodged in its bedrock.

With a sigh of pleasure Linda closed the door behind her and saw large, fluffy white bath-towels arranged near a bath that was sunk below the level of the floor. Along a tiled shelf stood jars of bath salts in a variety of colour and Linda chose the green one, her nostrils quivering to the aroma of pine when she removed the stopper. Oh yes, she would take a plunge in this sunken tub and the pine salts would refresh her body and her mind and she'd be able to view this overnight stay in a castle in a realistic way.

As she turned the mixer taps, shaped from crystal, Linda tried to believe that it was only imagination which made her feel as if she had fallen into the power of the man who owned all this. He had an air of dominance she was unused to, for her contact with men had been limited to professors of music, fellow students at the college, and Larry Nevins who wouldn't hurt a moth. For one brief hour she had been charmed by Don Ramos, but the meeting hadn't prepared her for someone like Karim el Khalid de Torres.

In a haze of pine and steam Linda removed her clothes and slid into the water; the tub was deep but she wasn't afraid of going under. She could swim and it really was a pleasure not to be confined to the narrow white limits of the bathtub at home where the slightest splash caused the water to slop over on to the floor.

Here she could kick about to her heart's content in water that felt divinely soft and fragrant.

How very rich the man must be, she thought. Did he own oil wells in Arabia, or was he a merchant prince whose merchandise was carried across the desert not upon the swaying back of camels as in days gone by, but in huge trucks?

Lost in speculations Linda didn't notice when the bathroom door opened to frame the tall, dark figure who filled her thoughts. 'So, there you are! Adoracion came to tell me that you had run away!'

Linda went as still as a marble nymph in a grotto, her eyes fixed upon him beneath the wet tangle of her hair. The pine-green water swayed around her pale figure, a hazy mirror that revealed to him every inch of her nudity. It was for Linda the second most devastating moment of her life but this time she didn't sink into merciful unconsciousness.

'I—I'm taking a bath,' she said nervously, her hand raking around for the big green sponge which had bounced out of her reach but would have been a belated shield from those penetrating eyes.

'So I see.'

'Y-you shouldn't be in here——' Linda could feel herself shrinking back against the marble surround of the bath, not knowing whether to conceal her front or her rear from his scrutiny. If only the pine crystals had been of the foaming sort then at least she'd have some cover from his gaze ... he was, after all, a stranger to her.

'I think you have bathed sufficiently for a young woman who has a multi-coloured bruise on her brow.' He took firm hold of one of the big white towels and came to the side of the sunken tub with it. 'Out with you, *bint*, before you come over dizzy again. You are in deep water!'

There was something in those words . . . some deep note of warning that almost turned Linda faint again. 'I—I can manage without your assistance,' she rejoined. 'If you think I'm coming out——'

'You are coming out!' He quite deliberately pulled the chain that released the plug and the water began to gush away at so rapid a pace that in less than a minute Linda knew she would be entirely revealed to him, without even a layer of translucent bath water to hide the shape of her. Rapidly she climbed the steps into the concealing folds of the extended towel and felt him wrap those folds closely about her wet body.

'There, was that so painful?' he murmured, and once again she seemed to hear desert gravel in his voice.

'I—I'm not used to having an audience while I take a bath,' she rejoined.

'That was immediately obvious.' His eyes were intent upon her face whose pallor was now flushed by his invasion of the bathroom. 'When Adoracion returned to the bedroom and you were no longer there, it didn't occur to her as it occurred to me that you would be taking a bath. You had been travelling and you felt hot and grubby, eh?'

She nodded and wished he would leave her alone to get dressed. She had never in her life felt so unbearably aware of herself in relation to a man, and her toes curled into the wool of the rug upon which she was standing. She was absolutely in his hands and no one in this household would question his behaviour, and afraid that her thoughts might show in her eyes Linda turned her head so her gaze fell upon his left hand, dark-skinned, strongly made, the intaglio crest of his ring catching her gaze . . . a falcon in ebony on gold.

'You are different,' he said, 'from many of the European women who come to sun their bodies on Spanish beaches. They have very little modesty and allow themselves to be used by hotel *servidors* as if it is some *cache*. *Ya*, I think you are very unlike them.'

He released her with those words and walked away from her to the door. 'I will see you later on.' As the door closed behind him Linda gave a shiver of reaction. The thick texture of the towel had dried her body and it certainly wasn't cold in the bathroom yet here she stood with her knees trembling. It was no use deluding herself . . . from the moment she had looked into the desert eyes of El Khalid she had felt threatened. Despite his vagrant resemblance to Don Ramos he was an entirely different sort of man, the Latin side of him almost overruled by the Arabian.

It was there in the hard-boned sculpture of his face; there in the inscrutable depths of his eyes shaded by brows and lashes dark as jet. He was a mixture of power, breeding and barbarism, and despite Linda's lack of sophistication it was the antenna of her femaleness which had searched him out.

She thought of the ring he wore, a falcon engraved upon gold. She almost felt again the firm grip of his capable looking hands. When he moved it was with a supple resilience she had never seen before in any human being, as if every joint and sinew of his large body was perfectly co-ordinated.

Anyway, she couldn't stay in here for the rest of the day, and discarding the bathtowel she quickly dressed herself, ran her fingers through her hair in an attempt to tidy it, then returned to the bedroom where the net curtains had been released to form a cool white pavilion around the bed.

Linda removed her shoes and lay on the bed in her skirt and blouse, as if hopeful that her English bought clothes would protect her from the strange and alarming sense of having been deprived of her freedom. The cobweb-fine nightwear still lay across the foot of the bed and try as she might Linda couldn't rid herself of the mental image of a masculine hand outlined beneath the pastel fabric.

With a fretful, weary restlessness Linda twisted back and forth on the bed, seeking the oblivion of sleep yet afraid of the helplessness of it. What if while she slept he came and stood at the bedside and let his eyes roam all over her? Oh God, her heart gave a thump at the very thought and for at least another half an hour she lay staring up at the white drapery, feeling not unlike a moth trapped in a net.

When sleep lays its touch across the eyes the sleeper is unaware and curled on her side Linda slept until the netting dimmed into a dusky veil, the lightness of her breathing the only sound in the big room where the long oval mirror reflected the moonlight when it came stealing through the window grilles.

A touch on the shoulder brought Linda awake from a surprisingly dreamless night, and dazedly she noticed that the netting no longer surrounded her and radiant sunlight was in the room and flickering on the coffee service which had been placed on the cabinet beside the bed. She glanced downwards feeling a weight across her body and found that the throwover covered her.

'*La señorita inglesa* is feeling much restored?'

Linda pushed herself into a sitting position and was relieved to find that she was still clad in her blouse and skirt. 'Yes, thank you,' she replied, and glanced around her in a surprised sort of way. 'Did I sleep all night?'

Adoracion inclined her severely groomed head where not a dark hair was out of place. 'Shall I pour the *señorita* a cup of coffee?'

'Yes, please!' Linda breathed the appetizing aroma, and as the details of her arrival here fell into place she smiled at the sunshine and thought how absurd she had been to suppose that her host had other than hospitable intentions towards her. Her headache was gone and today she would be able to go and see Dona Domaya.

'Did the men find my handbag?' she asked eagerly.

'Your coffee, *señorita*.' Adoracion placed the cup and saucer in Linda's hands and there was no telling from her face what thoughts were passing through her mind.

'Please tell me!' Linda felt suddenly afraid from the Spanish woman's demeanour that the news wasn't good.

'I think I must leave the *patron* to speak to you on the matter.' Adoracion moved away from the bedside. 'Your clothes are crumpled from sleeping in them so I will go and find replacements. The *señorita* is very slender so I would assume an English size ten?'

'Yes.' Linda wasn't bothered about clothing; she very much needed to know if her passport and official documents had been recovered. 'Please, you must have some idea—he won't mind if you tell me!'

'*El excelencia* would mind very much if I exceeded my orders.' Adoracion had a silent, almost gliding walk, and Linda had to watch her departure with a sense of frustration. His excellency was a tyrant, and as soon as she finished her coffee and visited the bathroom she would go and confront him. Oh yes, decidedly a man who liked to crack the whip over people, but she wasn't a member of his staff who had to be subservient to his orders.

She had finished her coffee and was on the point of going to the bathroom when Adoracion came back into the bedroom carrying garments over her arm. 'I hope these will meet with your approval, señorita.' They were displayed on the bed, a crisp white linen dress with a thin leather belt, a white slip edged with lace, a matching pair of briefs, and casual white shoes.

'Very nice,' Linda said gratefully. 'I was informed by your *patron* that clothing was kept in stock for people in transit from South America. Have there been many of them?'

'A considerable number, señorita, but now the troubles have quietened down we receive very few visitors—you are the first in quite some time.'

Linda picked up the white dress which had a crisply pleated skirt. It reminded her of sunny afternoons on the courts of Kingswood Country Club, the smack of tennis balls against the tautly strung rackets, and cool iced orange-juice in between the sets. 'Have you worked here at the *castillo* for a long time?' she found herself asking Adoracion.

'I was personal maid to the *patron's* mother,' came the reply. 'I was attendant upon her until the sad day she died. She never recovered, you see, from that dreadful day which became known as Black Saturday throughout the East. There was looting and plundering around the hotel where she and the Sheikh Khalid were staying for a while. A mob of men broke into their suite and the Sheikh was clubbed to death in front of that poor woman's demented eyes; she was but a shadow of herself for many weeks afterwards and she died in giving birth to her son, Karim el Khalid. In his favourite room in the *castillo* there hangs a portrait of her; a very beautiful woman whose memory he reveres by helping others as she was helped that terrible day of the riots in Palestine.'

It was a tragic story but for Linda it didn't alter her own impression of El Khalid. His hospitality was faultless, even down to a brand new toothbrush, but each time in his company she felt a strange disquiet. It was as if he touched upon instincts which she had been unaware of until that moment in his car when she found herself looking up at a brown face where distinction was at war with a deep strain of ruthlessness.

Perhaps something had entered into him that fearful day when his mother had been left amidst the wreckage of the room where her husband had been murdered in front of her. She had probably rocked the dead body in her arms, holding him crushed to her body where she carried his child.

Linda secured the slim leather belt of the white dress and studied her image in the oval mirror of the vast mahogany wardrobe. Apart from being a few inches too long it was a good fit, though the shoes were hopelessly too large. 'Here goes!' she thought, and stroked her fringe so that it almost concealed the bruise on her brow, too much a reminder that she was in the debt of this man who from a child had been heir not only to wealth but to the knowledge of cruelty. It had robbed him of both parents, and there seemed to Linda to be nothing remotely gentle left in the nature of Karim el Khalid de Torres.

Inexperienced as she was where men of the world were concerned, Linda sensed in her host a distinct lack of conventional behaviour. He lived by his own set of rules and probably snapped his fingers at the kind which had governed Linda's upbringing.

She fingered the tiny gold heart that was attached to her bracelet, which was inscribed with her mother's name, the truant Miriam who had run away all those years ago in order to live with an American who played the clarinet in a dance band. Linda's mother had been a singer with a London-based ensemble before giving up her career to become a wife and mother.

Linda felt sure that her own musical ability was inherited from her mother, a lively person so very different from Aunt Doris, with a vivaciousness Linda still remembered. Her abandonment had left a shattered man in charge of Linda and finally he had given in to his sister Doris and sent Linda to live with her and her husband in their perfectly run home where everything smelled of Mansion polish and always there were seasonal flowers on the glistening tops of veneered furniture.

By the time Linda was thirteen both her parents had vanished out of her life, but it was her mother with the sparkling brown eyes whom she missed the most. She, too, had lived by her own rules, and such rules didn't take into account the feelings of other people who might have their lives turned upside down.

It was true that Linda remembered her mother with affection but that didn't alter the fact that Miriam had chosen to please herself and in so doing had disrupted not only the life of her daughter but had left her devoted husband in total despair. Aunt Doris had never forgiven her and had tried her utmost to rid Linda of any fond thoughts relating to Miriam.

But love, as Linda realised, was a strange and abiding emotion, and often so strong that it could

survive the cruellest of blows. It sometimes made
Linda feel guilty that she still harboured affection for
her truant mother and failed to feel anything but
gratitude and a sense of duty towards Aunt Doris.

Her brow wrinkled as she gazed around this
handsome Spanish bedroom in which she had spent
the night. The trouble with Aunt Doris was that
everything shocked her if it wasn't rigidly conventional
... how unutterably shocked she would be to see her
niece in this strange situation ... beholden to a man
who hadn't a predictable bone in his body.

Unpredictable like the desert, Linda told herself,
where an unruffled surface was no indication of a
gathering storm. Again her fingers clenched the hard
little heart as she made her way along the sunshot
gallery to the stairs.

CHAPTER THREE

THE moment Linda set foot in the hall she was taken by a *servidor* to where the *patron* was taking breakfast on a sunlit patio beyond an archway framed in a mass of mauve bougainvillaea. He rose to his feet as she approached the table, clad in black riding breeches and a white silk shirt through which the darkness of his chest could be seen.

'*Bueños dias, señorita.*' He waited until she was seated then sat down again. 'You look as if a good night's sleep has done wonders for you—your head is quite clear and without pain this morning?'

'Yes, *señor*, sleep is a great healer.' Linda sat there tensely as she was served with an English breakfast of bacon, sausage and grilled tomatoes. The toast was golden and crisp, and clear honey gleamed in a jar. Everything looked appetising and part of her couldn't help but respond to such charming surroundings. As the aroma of coffee mingled with fresh toast and bacon Linda felt the need to satisfy her hunger.

After she had taken the edge off her hunger she glanced up from her plate and found the *patron* drinking coffee and frankly appraising her. 'I notice that Adoracion found you a suitable dress,' he remarked.

'Yes.' His remark seemed to invite the question she was clamouring to ask. 'Did your men manage to salvage my belongings, *señor*, in particular my handbag?'

'Unfortunately the sea is greedy,' he replied.

'You can't mean——?' Her heart seemed to sink into her midriff.

'I'm afraid I do mean it, *señorita*.' He spread his hands in a gesture of fatalism. 'But what is a handbag, what are a few official papers, you have your life ahead of you, have you not?'

'Of course.' She flushed, for he had managed to make her feel ungrateful, and for painful moments as she sat there she seemed to feel like the child whose aunt had constantly reminded her that she must always feel grateful for having relatives who took care of her because her parents had absconded from their duties. Linda had grown up in bondage to the word ingratitude.

'So what it means,' she took a quick swallow of coffee, 'is that I really have no right to be in Spain— not without my passport and visa?'

'You put it in a nutshell.' He made no attempt to spare her feelings. 'At this precise moment, *señorita*, you are a nomad as we say in the desert. A waif and stray without a penny to your name.'

Linda stared across the table at him, perhaps hoping to see a glimmer of sympathy in his eyes. Instead they were dark and impenetrable and they made her desperately aware of her aunt's warning that she would find herself among strangers whose ways were unfamiliar.

'Dona Domaya knows I'm here,' she said, a thread of panic in her voice. 'She and her brother will vouch for me . . .'

'Of a certainty, *señorita*, if they were here but Don Ramos has been obliged to take his sister back to the clinic in San Lopez from which she was discharged several weeks ago in the hope that she was cured of her depression. Alas, it began to reassert itself while they were on vacation in England where she was seen by a nerve specialist, and a message came from the *granja* yesterday afternoon that Ramos was very anxious and thought it best that she undergo further treatment.'

Linda gave a little shiver of desolation even as the Spanish sunlight stroked her arms with its warmth. Bees buzzed in the bougainvillaea and a brightly coloured bird spun among the trees; it was an idyllic scene and yet she felt as if something sinister was moving in her direction.

'Do have some fruit.' The deep voice broke in on her abstraction. 'Those nectarines are especially sweet and juicy—always it has seemed to me that in the garden of Eden it was a fruit more sensuous than the apple which tempted Eve to take a bite. What is your opinion, *señorita?*'

Linda gave him a look with a touch of fear in it. Why did it seem as if he could read her mind, or was the ability merely based on his worldliness? Such a man would have known many women so it wouldn't be all that difficult for him to see into the mind of someone like herself, who knew the movements of the cello bow far better than she knew the motivations of men.

'What has happened about Pepita?' she asked.

'The child has gone to San Lopez with her mother and her uncle. No doubt Ramos will find there a *dueña* for her.'

'I could take care of her as arranged——'

'No!' His voice cut Linda to silence. 'That is out of the question.'

'But why?' Linda sat very straight in her chair and defied his eyes. 'You're a man of influence and you could easily explain to the authorities why I'm without my working visa.'

'I could,' he agreed, and very carefully he was peeling a redflushed nectarine with a sharp-bladed silver knife, 'but I have no intention of doing so.'

'What an unfair thing to say!' Linda could hardly believe that he had said it. 'You—you're deliberately forcing me to stay here, aren't you?'

'Yes,' he said, imperturbably, and held towards her on the blade of the knife a section of the fruit. 'Take and taste.'

'I don't want it.'

'Don't be a child.'

Reluctantly she took the piece of fruit and placed it in her mouth; she chewed on it with the knowledge that he made her feel afraid of him. How did someone like herself fight a man whose shoulders stretched the fabric of his shirt and whose arms were corded with muscles that rippled beneath the hair-shadowed brown skin?

Yesterday she had felt that Don Ramos was within reach, but now he and his sister were no longer at the *granja* she was well and truly in the hands of El Khalid ... and he knew she was afraid of him, it was there in his manner, in the way he looked at her with eyes so dark the pupils were lost in them.

'If you are so set on being a *compañera*, then you can be mine,' he said, almost casually. 'I have been in need of one for some time and you will suit me very well.'

'You—you can't be serious?' Linda looked at him incredulously. 'I came here to work as a companion to a child not a man!'

'Your duties would be much the same.' He lounged back in his chair and slid a thin dark cigar between his lips. As he fired the tip from a gold lighter he studied Linda through the leaping flame, then the lighter clicked shut and was returned to his pocket. 'I like someone to read to me and I enjoy music—you were to teach Pepita the piano, I believe?'

'Yes, it's my favourite instrument next to the cello and I was informed by Don Ramos that there's a piano at the *granja*.'

'So you also play the cello?'

'Yes.'

'You are quite an accomplished young woman.'

'When it comes to music.'

'And when it comes to other things?' He smoked his cigar in a lazy manner, as if the matter of her employment was already settled and he had no intention of arguing with her. 'What other things are you good at, *señorita*?'

'I'm no good at being the kind of female companion you have in mind,' she retorted. 'Y-you have the most colossal nerve!'

'My intentions I assure you are strictly honourable.' Cigar smoke wreathed the dark, sardonic angles of his face. 'You speak of nerve and I say this to you, if you were chicken-hearted then you wouldn't be in my house at all. *Dios mio*, you would not sit facing me across this table, a rebellious woman I can deal with but not one with water in her veins, *comprende*?'

Yet her nerves were quivering like water when a rough wind passes over it and she felt her hands clench together in her lap, for there was something so adamant about the set of his features, as if he didn't even hear the word 'no' from a woman.

'First let me tell you a little about myself.' He studied for a brief moment the sharply burning point of his cigar. 'I am *soltero* which means that I have never felt the inclination to be married. On the other hand I am a man of property both here in Spain and in the Middle East and this means that I owe it to myself to have a son who will carry on my name and inherit my estate. This in every man is a basic desire and one I now wish to satisfy. So far as I'm concerned the emotions have nothing to do with my proposition. I am a man, *señorita*, who was born without any love in him. I have never in all my years met anyone who has filled my heart with boundless joy and I have very little interest in the phenomenon called love.'

He paused and allowed his eyes to play over Linda's face. 'I see in you, *la señorita inglesa*, a look of character, coolness and the need to fulfil an obligation, and so I am going to propose that you become the wife who will give me a child. I should prefer that child to be a son because in many ways the world is kinder to the male of the species, but it isn't an essential requirement. If the child is born a daughter then I shall be happy enough; there will be someone of my blood to inherit what is mine, but if I die a bachelor my estate will be divided up among relatives who will immediately start to argue about their share in case it yields a little less petroleum.'

Again he was looking at Linda with eyes that willed her submission to him. 'There are advantages to being the wife of a rich man; you will never need to take orders from an employer, you will be able to wear the very best clothes and jewellery, and best of all your marriage will be arranged by the head rather than the foolish heart which so often leads people astray so they find themselves on the path of thorns rather than the path of primroses.'

He raised his cigar to the ironic curve of his lips and drew on it until the end glowed fiercely.

Out of all those words one sentence seemed to burn itself into Linda's mind. Without a flicker of emotion on his face he had told her that he was a man who had been born without any love in him, and her reaction to these words had been strange and quite unexpected ... she had felt a thrill of compassion which had seemed to run from the nape of her neck all the way down her spine to her thighs. It was a feeling she had never experienced before, and her mind jolted away from the sexual aspects of it.

No, she didn't want to believe that she was excited by the thought of being this man's wife ... a man who freely admitted that he had no love to give anyone and whose wish for parenthood was based on his need to pass on his worldy goods to a child of his body.

'Is a man who can't feel love a fit person to be a parent?' she asked quietly.

He shrugged his wide shoulders and flicked ash from his cigar, a gesture that seemed to underline his attitude. 'Possibly not in sentimental terms, but we live in a commercial world and wealth has its compensations. I can give a wife every luxury and a child every advantage and who is to say that these assets don't count in a world where adultery and divorce have become commonplace? Both in Spain and the Arab states the arranged marriage has been proved to have its advantages.'

'Then why, *señor*, don't you take a Spanish girl for your wife, or an Arabian girl? Why ask a perfect stranger to marry you?' There was a look of gravity in Linda's eyes as she regarded him; even yet she couldn't take his proposal seriously. They knew very little about each other beyond the fact that he was rich and she at this precise moment was without a penny to her name. If he wanted to buy a woman then why didn't he choose a Latin beauty with dark glowing hair and romantic brown eyes; or a girl of the East skilled in all the ways of pleasing a man?

'It's true,' he said, 'that the world is filled with ambitious beauties who would leap at the chance of being a rich man's wife, but you have three essential qualities which, to be frank, I find captivating. You are British and I have never met one who isn't courageous. I admire the ability to make music, and above all I know you are a virgin.'

That evocative word hung on the warm air between them, and then a bee buzzed loudly in the cup of a pale pink flower and Linda saw a smile on the edge of his mouth.

'Do I embarrass you?'

'N-no.'

'I believe I do, and that is another indication that you may have given yourself to your music but you have never given yourself to a man. You see, *berida*, it wouldn't suit me in the least to have other than an absolute virgin for my wife.'

'You seem absolutely sure that I am one, El Khalid.' Linda endured the scrutiny of his dark and worldly eyes and felt her body tingle with the most comprehensive blush of her life. 'I do happen to have a boy friend back home in England.'

'You must long to be with him,' he said sarcastically. 'Your presence here in Spain proves how much you enjoy his company.'

'Englishmen don't mind if their girl friends work abroad for a while—and absence makes the heart grow fonder, *señor*.'

'I doubt it.' He ground out his cigar stub as he spoke. 'I daresay there is a young man in England who would like to marry you—you are pleasing to look upon with your honey-coloured hair and your topaz eyes. I daresay the young man yearns to have you but I see a young woman whose feelings are too cool and cloistered to have ever felt the passion of a man. You are unawakened and I know it!'

Abruptly he leaned across the table and locked her gaze into his. 'I wonder if you realise how completely in my power you are? I could have you, *berida*, without the benefit of a marriage service.'

The iron chill of his words went all the way through her even as she sat there in a web of sunlight that made such a contrast of her fairness and his darkness.

'Don't be anxious,' he mocked, 'if you are going to give me a child then I prefer that all the legal knots be tied so there is no likelihood of the courts ever disputing the rights and privileges of my son or daughter.'

'You seem to be taking it for granted that I'll marry you.' The words felt strange on her lips, for she had known this man less than twenty-four hours but with his fatalistic nature he seemed to attach significance to the way they had met . . . as if the hand of kismet had thrown that sack of vegetables on the road and caused her cab to swivel above an abyss of rocks and ocean.

'You owe me something for saving your life,' he said in answer to her thoughts. 'A life for a life, let us say?'

'You must want a son and heir very badly, El Khalid.' Linda's heart was drumming in her breast and once again she experienced a kind of compassion for this man who seemed to have everything but love. 'How can you know what I'm like? I might be a selfish and mercenary shrew who will take everything and give nothing in return. I mean, is it wise to judge a book from the cover?'

'Perhaps not wise but certainly intriguing and I would consider myself a tame specimen of a man if I had failed to notice how shocked you were when I walked in upon you taking a bath. When I saw you groping for the sponge I thought you were going to aim it at my head.'

'I wish I'd thought of it.' She flushed anew at the glints of sardonic amusement in his eyes.

'Were you seeking it in order to try and conceal yourself from my wicked gaze?'

She glanced away from him, the fair skin of her face burning beneath his gaze. 'I—I think this game has gone far enough, *señor*. As there's no place for me at the *granja* then I would be grateful if you would lend me the money so I can fly home to England.'

'There is ample room for you at the *castillo*, or if you prefer we can go to Morocco and live in my desert house—the house of the nightingales because in the days of colonial rule a religious nursing order resided there.'

'Don't keep assuming that I'll marry you.' Linda was beginning to feel as if her wishes were bouncing against a stone wall. 'I've no intention of living in Morocco with you—I want to go home.'

'You sound like a child instead of a grown woman.' His eyes narrowed dangerously. 'I am doing the courteous thing, I'm suggesting that you become my wife before I take you to bed. You are at liberty to make a choice but I feel it will make you happier with yourself if you come to me as a bride rather than a mistress.'

'Y-your arrogance is beyond belief—you really mean the things you're saying to me and I'm supposed to let you have your way.' Linda could see from his face that he had quite set his mind on having his own way where she was concerned. She was to satisfy his urge to become a parent and love was to play no part in the production of his child. His paramount requirement was that she be a virgin, and a single look at his firmly set jaw was enough to inform Linda that she could scream her head off and still he would proceed with his purpose.

'I saved you from a broken neck,' he reminded her. 'Don't you think you owe me something in return?'

'Y-you ask a lot of me, El Khalid.'

'I wonder what upsets you so?' He scanned her face mercilessly. 'Would you prefer a pack of sentimental lies? Would you be more agreeable if I claimed to have fallen in love with you?'

'N-no.'

'No?' he mocked. 'Come, I know enough about your sex to know how susceptible you are to the word love. You regard it as the password to paradise and that's why the Don Juans of this world use it so frequently and with such success. It has been the open sesame to the bedroom since time began and had I used it in conjunction with my proposal you would be responsive to me instead of resistant. No matter. I've offered you a choice.'

'Some choice!' she exclaimed.

'It's better than none.'

'Why me?' Linda looked defiant. 'I'm not greedy for your money—it won't soften me. But what you can be sure of is that I'll hate you if you force yourself on me. Is that what you perversely want, to be hated instead of loved by the woman you marry?'

'I ask neither for love nor hate,' he rejoined. 'I ask for your co-operation in a venture and you will be amply rewarded—ah, you wrinkle the pert nose but I know a little more of the ways of people than you, *la señorita inglesa* with your sentimental notion that being a companion in a Spanish household is an occupation of fulfilment. A companion is no more than being a *servidor* minus the uniform, and that you should seek it, a girl with musical ability, is a thing of amazement to me and I can but assume that you had a basic need to escape your life in England.'

Linda felt her pulses jolt, for once again he seemed to have delved into her mind with those eyes that saw everything and gave nothing away, and suddenly she could sit there no longer and leaping to her feet she ran towards one of the flagstoned paths that led among the palm trees and the flowering shrubs that dropped their petals lazily on the pathway.

It was inevitable that he would pursue her but still she gave a broken cry when his strong hands closed on her shoulders and he swung her so effortlessly to face him. In the dappled sunlight they confronted each other and Linda felt that in the white dress she was like some palpitating moth which beat its wings in a vain effort to fly away.

'Where do you think you are going?' he asked. 'How far do you think you can get?'

'You're abominably sure of yourself, aren't you?' She tried to break free but was held firmly by his hands that were swarthy against the fabric of her dress. His face above her was masterful, sure of itself and more than a touch untameable. He had her, Linda realised, and he wasn't going to let go of her.

'*Ay*, I'm sure of what I want,' he agreed. 'You are wildly uncertain and I accept that, but of a certainty you came to Spain in search of something you were unable to find in your own country—if it was adventure then look upon this marriage as such. To each other we are unexplored territory and who knows what we shall find in each other's company.'

'All I expect to find is tyranny and arrogance,' she rejoined . . . and something she was not prepared for, a tingling awareness of his touch that extended from her shoulders to every vulnerable part of her body. The backs of her knees seemed to weaken and it was beyond her own belief that she could feel such sensations for a man who seemed to have feelings tipped with the steel of the Spanish *banderilla*, that awful weapon used in the bullring to weaken the brave bull until finally it capitulated to the sword.

It seemed that she was on the point of capitulation, driven by weaknesses in her own body which she had never suspected. Those few bashful hugs and kisses she had received from Larry Nevins had left her totally unaffected ... but the touch of Karim el Khalid de Torres was another matter and as Linda realised it she tried to wrench herself away from him.

In reaction he pulled her hard against him and even as her lips parted in protest he took them in a kiss which bore no relation to those dry, hurried kisses which Larry had aimed at her mouth rather than directed with such force and urgency that Linda lost awareness of everything except the savage movements that didn't penetrate the silky skin of her lips but set them burning.

She vaguely knew it was expertise and not the hungry desire of a man driven by his emotions but— oh God—to feel such kisses on other parts of her! To feel these sensations magnified! She mustn't dare yield to feelings which had nothing to do with love! This was sheer animal appeal which she felt in the powerful arms whose skin seemed to burn against her body, awakening a response from her deep inner self which threatened to overwhelm her.

'Don't!' She almost ricked her neck as she made the effort to turn her head aside from his mouth.

'Don't you enjoy the lovemaking of a man who knows his business?' He spoke mockingly against the side of her neck, where the heart's vein beat its wild message against his lips.

'This has nothing to do with love—you said that love was something you could never feel.' Even as she spoke Linda could feel her body pressed close to his, to a warm strength and suppleness that made her head spin and her breath come quickly. Things were happening inside her which were beyond her control ... her body seemed detached from her mind and was making its own urgent demands. Her skin quivered in the most acutely sensitive way as she felt a warm hand slide over the curve of her hip.

'I like the feel of your body,' he murmured. 'I like its young slenderness and most of all the fact that I am the first man in your life to touch you in this way. I know it and feel it! You are completely unawakened and the thought of being the man who awakens you is an incentive I fully intend to pursue.'

As he said the words he released her and watched as she instinctively sought the support of a nearby palm-tree whose rough stem penetrated the fabric of her dress. There she stood with her hands gripping the roughness, the pupils of her eyes so wide that the irises were like rings of gold around them.

'You look,' a smile seemed to touch his mouth and then was gone, 'like a wild young falcon who has flown into my covet after a long journey which has left you exhausted. Why fight yourself, *berida*? We both know when you opened your eyes yesterday and found yourself in my arms that it was more than a mishap which caused us to meet. For some time I had been wishing to marry and you suit my requirements in every respect.'

'W-what if you don't suit mine?' she managed to say despite the wild thumping of her heart.

'A mere bagatelle.' He snapped his fingers. 'If you returned to England you might marry this young man who obviously has no hold on your emotions. Young women don't turn their backs on someone who excites them and though I'm fully aware that you would rather be tortured than admit it, I know that a part of you is very excited by the prospect of belonging to me. You shake your head but I know!'

'No.' She was saying it to convince herself rather than him. '*No.*'

'Yes.' He stepped close to her and deliberately pressed her to the palm-tree with his body; she quivered and her eyelids sank down as if to hide the desire in her eyes. 'Don't!'

'You might as well eliminate that word from your vocabulary,' he softly mocked, 'because it just doesn't exist between us.'

'I—I don't love you——'

'Love,' he brought his lips close to hers, 'is another word without meaning so far as you and I are concerned. How soft your skin, how bright your hair, how delicately strong the feel of your hipbones. You will give me a beautiful child, *berida*, and that is what counts. Is it not better to be the mother of your own child rather than the *compañera* of a stranger's offspring?'

'Please——'

'When you say please your lips shape themselves for a kiss.' And he lowered his dark head and once again Linda was at his mercy and powerless to resist the potent discovery that she liked the bold texture of his mouth and the feelings that erupted inside her when his fingers roamed over her skin. She had to grip the stem of the palm-tree very hard because of themselves her arms wanted to enclose his shoulders and her fingers wanted to touch him.

She felt dazed by the sensations he made her feel . . . shocked by the realisation that this stranger had managed to get closer to her in twenty-four hours than anyone she had known for years. Ruthlessly he had stepped across the border of her reserve and taken her totally by surprise.

Linda looked at him in a lost way and saw in his eyes his awareness that she was losing the will to resist him. Up until now her body had been only an instrument for making lovely sounds on the cello but he had let loose in her a disharmony between mind and emotion . . . he had made her aware of what lay hidden behind her façade of coolness.

She wanted to be cool and controlled but instead she could feel the agitated rise and fall of her breasts tautly brushing the hard wall of El Khalid's chest.

'I think you will marry me,' he said, and there was a heaviness to his eyelids as he regarded her. 'I think your resistance to the idea is already beginning to melt.'

'I—I barely know you,' she protested. 'I can't let you take over my life in this high-handed way!'

'Why can't you? The exploration of unknown territory can be exciting.' He pressed closer to her and his body made vibrant contact with hers, and a smile glimmered in his eyes when she gave a little gasp . . . then another, the pupils of her eyes large and burning.

'Don't make me,' she implored huskily. 'You're deliberately using your position to get me to do what you want.'

'Of course I am,' he said shamelessly. 'Why not admit that you like the idea. Two people with only themselves to please; a man and a woman ready for marriage.'

No . . . it was madness and she had to fight him.

'Let me go!' She pushed at his shoulders and found them firm and unyielding. 'I want to go home to my family in England—my aunt warned me about coming here, she said I'd land myself in trouble——'

'A lady of foresight,' he drawled. 'I think it's fair to remind you that my arrival on the road yesterday prevented you from being flown home to England in a box.'

Linda shuddered at the images he evoked. 'You're using emotional blackmail in order to coerce me and you're quite ruthless about it—quite heartless!'

'And quite candid.' He took hold of her hand and pressed it to his chest where the beat of his heart was firm and regular. 'My heart is just a machine inside my body; it has never been disturbed by the emotion people refer to as love. I had no mother or father to love when I was a child. I grew up knowing my mother's face only from a portrait and so I never learned to eagerly await her arrival in my nursery morning and night. I never breathed her perfume or felt her kiss on my face. I was in the hands of people paid to take care of me, then later on I was sent to a school where boys were taught to be self-reliant to the point of harshness. From there I entered a military academy and in my first year there was a war in the Middle East and I became a soldier who killed his enemies and saw his comrades killed or injured.'

He paused as if to let his words sink right into Linda's mind. 'I want my own child to know its mother, and I want the mother of that child to be loved by him. I don't ask for your love but I see in you a capacity to feel it and I am ruthless enough to take you now—here and now among the palm trees and believe me when I let you out of my arms, *berida*, you will have my child inside you!'

Words spoken with such iron savagery they left Linda reeling with shock ... never would she have believed that one day she would hear a man say such a thing to her. Her life until now had protected her from the kind of sexual threat that was almost cruelly apparent on his face.

Her eyes raced over his face, seeing there the power and the virility and the threat. Nerves deep inside her body seemed to clutch at her to the point of pain and suddenly she swayed forward and found herself pressed to the hard warmth of his chest. She breathed that warmth and the tang of his cigar smoke and felt her faintness begin to recede.

'I—I don't know how to fight you,' she said helplessly.

'Just stop trying.' His fingers threaded her hair and stroked the nape of her neck. 'You weren't made for fighting, you were made for more sensitive skills and the time has come to apply them. It's as simple as that.'

No, she thought, no involvement with such a man could be a simple matter. She moved her restless head against him and winced with pain when her bruised brow made contact with his flesh and bone. 'You overpower me with the things you say——'

'Because I have swept aside the polite chit-chat of strangers?' There was amusement in his voice. 'Are we strangers when we kiss?'

Linda found herself making a negative movement with her head. When he kissed her all reasoning fled and she was aware only of impulse, and urgings that seemed incredible to her. How could she feel such needs ... was it possible they were related to the blow on her head? Had something gone wrong so she was no longer the person she had been? A girl of cool composure who adored music and loved romantic poetry and held in her heart her shy image of the *parfait chevalier*.

That perfect knight had never resembled in any way the man who held her in his arms right now . . . a man who had told her with brutal candour that he had no capacity for love.

'You say words—make images that confuse me,' she breathed. 'I feel—trapped.'

'A quail in the net, eh?' He held her away from him and his eyes seemed to strip away the white dress from her body that shrank for an instant and then felt desirous of what he made her feel when he looked at her . . . he didn't need Arab cloak, head ropes and leather boots; even without them he was every inch the sun lord who fought his enemies without a stab of fear, and took a woman without a spark of love.

'A tender quail ready for the plucking,' he laughed, and Linda gazed in fascination at the dazzle of his white teeth against his sun darkened skin.

'My aunt,' she exclaimed, 'I have to let her know——'

'The two of you have a sympathetic relationship?' he demanded.

'Of course——'

'I think that isn't quite true,' he contradicted. 'Young as you look, you are beyond the age of needing permission to marry so I think it best that we proceed to suit ourselves. You came to Spain, did you not, in order to live your own life?'

'Yes,' she agreed, a flash of temper in her eyes. 'I did come here to live my own life but I didn't get very far before you took charge of me!'

'I feel certain,' the edge of his teeth glimmered, 'that you will find life with me a little more exciting than you found it with your aunt. Your eyes, my child, are easy for me to read and when you mentioned the woman they became shadowed—I assume she has been your guardian?'

'She and my uncle,' Linda admitted. 'They've been good to me but Aunt Doris can be difficult. She has always made me feel duty bound and so in the end I just had to get away, especially when——'

'When?' he encouraged.

Linda shrugged her shoulders. She had been about to mention Larry Nevins and the pressure that was being put upon her to marry him. 'When I decided to work abroad instead of joining an orchestra. I adore music but I—I always wanted to be a soloist and I fall short of perfection.'

'Don't we all,' he drawled. 'You shall be my soloist, *mia* Linda. You will play exclusively for me—in all ways.'

Linda wanted to defy him but he sealed off the words before she could speak them, gathering her close to the hard threat and promise of his body, making her aware once again that they were strangers until they touched, until they kissed.

'We shall go East to be married,' he said decisively. 'To the desert where the sands have a timeless magic and where the moon is a honey ball at its fullest. This plan is agreeable to you?'

'I seem to have no choice, El Khalid.'

'True.' His smile was without shame. 'Any resistance from you would be dealt with.'

'How?' she wanted to know, a hint of resistance in the tilt of her chin.

'You have heard of the poppy, haven't you?'

She felt a stab of shock. 'You wouldn't—dare.'

'Try me,' he challenged.

Linda studied the sculpture of his face and looked into the dark eyes that were like nightfall and she knew his threat was no empty one. 'You would do it, wouldn't you—like some white slaver you'd drug me!'

'Yes.' For endless moments his gaze seemed to penetrate to the far reaches of her body. 'There are many things between a man and a woman that will always be primitive and I see no virtue in making myself out to be a gentle man.'

'I—I think you might be a wicked man,' she breathed.

'Wicked,' he mocked, 'just because I advocate that when women try on the trousers it's up to the men to pull them off, *pronto*. Women at heart want to be mastered.'

'Is that what I shall have, *señor*, a master?'

'Did you ever doubt it, *berida*?'

'I don't like the thought of being bullied.'

'I'm more subtle than a bully, my girl.'

'I hope so.'

'Be sure of it, *doncella*.'

Linda was sure of nothing where this man was concerned; the only certainty was that he took what he wanted. 'That word you used—I haven't heard it before. What does it mean?'

'It means virgin, which is what you are, eh?'

'What would you do if I wasn't a virgin?' Her eyes held a deep gravity as they dwelt on his face where the bones thrust proudly beneath the naturally dark skin.

'Feel cheated,' he replied.

'Then don't you think you should marry a girl of your own country?'

'Perhaps so,' he spoke almost callously, 'but I happen to want you.'

'To be your willing slave?'

'Why not?' He gave a brief laugh. 'Deep down in women there is such an urge but they tend to fight against it. The world might be a more pleasant place if women gave in gracefully to the fact that it's their bodies that delight men, not their arguments. Women are at their most delightful when they surrender themselves body and soul to a man. They are the gateway to passion and men turn the key.'

'Wisdom of the East?' she asked.

'Of course.' A smile flicked his lip, and his hand pressed its warmth against the white fabric of her dress, his fingertips lightly touching the young curve of her breast.

A thrill of fear and excitement made itself felt deep inside her; Linda's every instinct informed her that El Khalid was a man of powerful passions. Everything about him was so utterly vigorous and evident in the thick darkness of his hair, in the mahogany warmth of his skin, in the deep timbre of his voice.

Linda couldn't deny the excitement which his touch aroused in her and she felt herself inclining towards his dominance, surrendering to whatever he demanded of her. 'Don't completely scare me,' she pleaded. 'Leave me with a few illusions.'

'Romantic ones?' he mocked. 'I want you and that is a reality, girl with the hair gold like the tinting in old Koranic script.'

'Oh——' She caught her breath, defenceless when he chose to charm her.

'But every coin has its reverse,' he added. 'A sweet, cool face can hide scorpions.'

This time Linda looked at him aghast, and holding her gaze he bent his head and kissed her mouth. 'Don't worry,' he murmured, 'you are more than likely to be the one who gets stung.'

'Yes, damn you.' Her eyes blazed defiance into his. 'You're as hard as ox-leather!'

'And you are soft as silk, *mia lindo*.'

Soft, vulnerable ... trapped, she thought, and dazedly wondered if she was dreaming this man and this moment. But no—no dream of hers had ever contained a figure so vigorously real. When she blinked her eyes he didn't drift away like smoke in the air, taking with him the things he had said.

The only dreamlike factor was that she seemed powerless to prevent the events taking place. When she tried to run his arms were there to prevent her. When she tried to protest he stopped the words with his warm demanding mouth. There seemed nothing she could do, and when she looked at him she saw herself trapped in the darkness of his eyes.

'Say yes to me,' he insisted.

'N-no——'

'Say it or else.'

Slowly, deliberately, she could feel his hand mounting her body, pressing into her waist, travelling upwards until it enclosed her left breast. She quivered helplessly as he stared down into her eyes. She felt him toying with her and saw something creeping into his eyes that warned her it was now ... now among the palms, down on the ground, without a stitch of dignity.

'Damn you—yes!'

'*Bueno!*' And with the strength that snatched her breath he swung her by the waist until she hung above him and then with a kind of savage pleasure he kissed her body through the fabric of her dress and she heard him say: '*Mia joya!*"

'You're crazy,' she gasped.

'As a loon.' He lowered her to her feet. 'Now come with me and I shall put a bracelet on you.'

'I have a bracelet.'

He lifted her left hand and gave the wristlet a cursory glance. 'A memento of your schooldays, eh? The one I have locked in my safe is pure lustrous gold—I discovered it in Morocco and I never knew why I bothered to buy it. Now I have the answer, for it is the Spanish custom to give a *novia* a bracelet rather than a ring.'

'You're far more of an Arab, El Khalid.'

He shot down at her his wickedly glimmering smile. 'Afraid that I am going to shut you up in my *harem*?'

'Aren't you?' she murmured.

'There does happen to be one in my desert house.'

Linda felt his firm possession of her hand . . . a possession that in a very short time would extend to the rest of her. Not with love, nor with the tenderness of two people who had grown close together in a courtship. She and El Khalid were going to be strangers at the altar. In just a few minutes she was going to accept his golden shackle on her wrist.

She could hardly believe in her own actions . . . she, Linda Layne who had always been a girl of sensibility.

CHAPTER FOUR

LINDA trailed her fingers over the fabric of her dress which was beautifully silky to the touch and in a honey colour that was complimented by her coat, a dark sable lined with silk. Karim had insisted on giving her the coat, just as he'd insisted that she call him by his first name ... still as strange on her tongue as the realisation that she was flying with him to Fez Eldjid.

The costly beauty of her dress and coat didn't suppress the qualms she felt, for in the opposite seat of this privately owned aircraft Karim sat with a withdrawn look, plunged deep in his thoughts and hardly aware of her.

She had stopped pretending to herself that she wasn't drawn to him physically and through the veil of her lashes she admired him in the smooth brown suit and white-on-white shirt where at the cuffs there was the dark gleam of onyx studs.

In a mental sense, however, she felt no closer to him than on the day they had met and yet here she was, flying with him to Fez where they were going to become husband and wife. In expensive luggage stowed on the aircraft there was a trousseau of lovely clothes which, bought in Barcelona at one of the best houses of fashion, had replaced the less glamorous garments she had lost. Struck speechless, Linda had heard Karim inform the manageress that his *novia* was to be supplied with sets of lingerie, evening and day dresses, blouses, skirts and shoes in assorted styles, and riding and leisure wear.

'You have a fortunate *novia*,' the woman had smiled.

'He's buying me,' Linda thought to herself, 'and I'm no longer struggling.'

It wasn't that she was seduced by the lovely clothes, or by the lustrous bracelet on her wrist ... during those last few days in Spain she had often felt a stab of doubt, but she knew that what held her to her promise was the man himself.

Insidiously he had cast his spell over her and the prospect of being his wife was more exciting than the thought of going home to the mock-Tudor house in Essex where, once again, the mock-smartness of the suburban life would engulf her in its routines and its attitudes. In such an environment it wasn't possible to be an individual. Within her age group the girls and women wore a duplication of each others' clothing and hairstyles. There was a sameness about the people that imitated the sameness of the streets and houses, and within those houses each family lived a life that was suffocatingly similar to the life of the family next door.

Linda had chosen the unknown devil rather than the one she knew, and there he sat in the dark and brooding shape of Karim el Khalid de Torres.

She recalled how he had told the woman in the fashion house that he admired the colour of his *novia*'s hair and wanted the fabrics chosen for her to compliment her colouring.

Her hand stole upwards and she fingered the bright wings of hair beneath the small close hat that she wore; a dark-honey cloche that reflected the colour of her eyes.

'You are perfection.' Karim spoke abruptly. 'The perfect travelling companion for a man; for you to sit with your thoughts and leave me to consider mine.'

Her lashes fluttered, for he had startled her, and she

gave him an uncertain smile. 'Your thoughts looked like very deep ones, *señor*.'

'Do you plan to address me so formally when we are married?' he asked, a faint glimmer of mockery in his eyes . . . eyes dark as the studs that secured the cuffs of his shirt.

'I shan't know until we are—married.' Still the word could induce her heart to give a little trip, like a toe stubbing itself on a staircase that led to a mysterious room. Much of Karim was locked away in that secret room and Linda still felt afraid of marital revelations. They would come, those revelations, for a woman couldn't live with a man without discovering what he chose to conceal before the intimacy of marriage.

'Are you excited by the idea of being married in Fez?'

'Amazed is a better word,' she replied. 'I look out of this window beside me and realise I'm up in the clouds instead of firmly down on the ground in sensible shoes.'

A remark which caused him to glance at her slender legs and feet in beautifully fitting two-toned court shoes. 'You have a glamour, *mia*, that was concealed by your plain suit and your sensible footwear, and I feel rather like an explorer who has uncovered a work of art. Tomorrow when we face the *Ma'zoun* I feel sure you will be a revelation.'

'Is the ceremony a complicated one?' Linda was curious as well as apprehensive, and unsurprised that he wished their marriage to be conducted by an Arabian priest. He was an Arab himself on his father's side and a small voice whispered in her mind that it was comparatively easy for a man of the East to become disentangled from a wife he no longer wanted.

He had been candour itself where she was concerned, he wanted to father a child and that was his sole reason for taking a wife. In the event that she gave him a child he might well decide that she was expendable. It was, in a way, something Linda expected to happen despite what he had said about wanting his child to grow up in the care of a loving mother.

The one thing she was sure of where Karim was concerned was that he was unpredictable. He had sprung upon her that shopping spree in Barcelona, and also the fact that he had decided on an Arabian wedding.

'You will enjoy the ceremony.' He sat lighting a cigar, the rise and fall of the flame playing over the dark authority of his face. 'There is nothing at all to be nervous about and I have sent word ahead that I'm marrying a girl of the West but I would, of course, like it if you will agree to be dressed in the traditional Eastern way. Would you mind so much?'

Linda considered his question, then shook her head. 'Brides in England wear a veil and a long dress so really there isn't all that much difference, is there?'

Cigar smoke slid from his lips ... those bold lips that sent tiny shivers through Linda whenever she looked at his mouth. His dark eyes strayed over her slightly pensive face.

'I'm gratified that you are being so composed about everything, Linda. Your mind is now more at ease, eh? You don't see it as so strange that you and I are going to enter into marriage together despite our short acquaintance?'

'I—I still get the odd butterfly just here.' She pressed a hand to her midriff and drew his eyes to her slim figure in the dress that clung softly to the shape of her. His gaze moved downward and rested on her right leg, lightly crossed over her left leg so her foot swung with a giveaway touch of nerves.

'We have a custom in the East of giving a gold anklet and I have it with me. Tomorrow I would like you to wear it—now don't look outraged, it isn't a shackle but a delicate chain and let us say it amuses me to give in now and then to my Arabian impulses in the matter of my woman.'

Linda caught her breath, for his voice seemed to dwell on the words. Did she really know what she was doing in relation to this man? Even in a well-cut, modern styled suit he looked like a man who had wandered into the wrong century.

'Will you be wearing an Eastern outfit tomorrow?' she asked.

'Of a certainty.' He drew on his cigar and a ring of smoke sailed in the air between them. 'I tend to wear the insignia of a Sheikh when I participate in a ceremony of importance. You do realise that I am a Sheikh?'

She smiled uncertainly. 'Who would have dreamed that an ordinary English girl like myself would be marrying a man of title—shall I have a title as well?'

He inclined his head. 'The people of my household will address you as *lellah* which means lady. By this time tomorrow you will have become the Lady Linda.'

'Oh——' Her lips quivered visibly. 'You're marrying me, Karim, without knowing a great deal about me.'

'I know about you what I consider essential.' His eyes possessed her in a comprehensive look. 'If you could see yourself as I see you then you would understand.'

'Fine feathers make fine birds,' she said wryly. 'I know I'm not beautiful—I have a tilt to my nose, my mouth is too wide and my hair isn't the dark Latin kind that seems so manageable.'

'But all put together they make an appealing combination.' He leaned forward and his fingers closed around her suspended right ankle, a gesture that sent a thrill running up her leg . . . he knew, just as she did, that his touch had an effect upon her she was helpless to control. Whatever her doubts he could erase them just by laying his hand upon her and right now she was mesmerised by his fingers as they stroked the silky slenderness of her leg.

'Your body sets fire to me,' he murmured. 'I want every inch of your white skin, every soft golden hair, every pulse beat. It's enough for both of us to know, that we aren't strangers when we touch.'

Was it really enough, Linda thought, as he leaned back in his seat and conferred with the steward about their lunch. Some wild and irresistible force had driven her into the arms of Karim el Khalid de Torres, for she could have sworn that she would never marry anyone unless convinced that she madly loved the man and was loved by him.

'Chilled champagne with pure orange juice, *lellah*?' Karim's voice broke in amusedly upon her deep thoughts.

'Oh—yes, please.'

'A malt whisky for me,' Karim informed the steward, who gave him a polite bow and moved away along the carpeted aisle to the pantry.

'I notice you aren't an orthodox Arab,' Linda remarked.

He shook his head. 'I have never pretended to be either saint or sinner, I am just a man with the usual set of vices and virtues.'

A man, she thought, who had never broken his heart

over anyone; who was highly capable of giving a woman joy as well as suffering. It was all there in his forceful face ... unspoken on the boldly formed lips whose kisses silenced her questions but not her doubts.

'While you were sitting spellbound I ordered lunch,' he said. 'I think I have an idea what pleases your taste buds.'

She flushed slightly for he had a way of imbuing some of his remarks with a sensuality that made her quiver as she could make the cello quiver when she drew the bow across its sensitivity as if she were a finely tuned instrument in his hands.

'What have you ordered?' she asked.

'Truffles poached in wine, pepper butter, melted on steaks with an assortment of vegetables, and deep gooseberry pie and cream.'

'Mmm, sounds delicious.'

'Delicious,' he murmured, and his eyes were on her lips, his eyelids heavy and thoughtful. 'What were you thinking a while ago?'

'Oh, that I'm not sure if I'm awake or dreaming— everything has happened so quickly.'

'You feel as if I've dragged you aboard this aircraft?'

'Something like that.'

'By the hair?' He reached forward and removed her hat, throwing it aside with a careless disregard for the money it had cost.

'Don't do that to my lovely little hat,' she reproved him, picking it up and stroking a dent out of the suede. 'Don't you like it?'

'I prefer to see your hair.' His gaze stroked the goldy softness of it, framing her face in the pageboy style she had never changed from the age of sixteen when in a mood of defiance she had gone to a local hairdresser and asked him to cut off the braids her aunt insisted upon. Aunt Doris had always wanted to keep her a schoolgirl who would stay young and obedient and not develop the whims and passions of a woman.

Heaven alone knew what Aunt Doris' reaction would be when she received the letter which Linda had posted off to England from Barcelona. She would probably have one of her vapours and poor Uncle Henry would have to revive her and then listen for hours while she went on and on about the ingratitude of the younger generation. Well, it couldn't be helped. Here she was with her husband-to-be and they were high in the air, being served drinks from the steward's tray.

'Mmm, this is nice.' She watched the bubbles spilling through the orange tinted champagne. 'What luxury!'

Karim laughed in that deep-throated way of his. 'What an ingenuous young creature you are, Linda.'

'Very naïve, I expect, by comparison to some of your woman friends.'

'A breath of fresh air is welcome after the cloy of perfume—yes, you are a girl unexpectedly different from anyone I ever knew before.'

'I—I expect you've known lots of women.'

'Thousands,' he mocked. 'Young woman, I have been busy with things apart from the pleasures—do you imagine I keep a selection of houris in my desert house, who await my arrival with panting bosoms and hungry eyes rimmed in kohl?'

'I hope you don't,' she replied.

'You want to be my one and only woman?'

She nodded. 'Karim—everything is going to be all right, isn't it? We are strangers in so many ways . . .'

'But not in the way that counts.' His eyes compelled her to agree with him. 'If either of us sought comfort and cosiness then we wouldn't be together right now—those are not the requirements of either of us so be honest with yourself.'

It was true, she couldn't doubt the excitement his touch aroused in her ... she could no longer deny that she wanted to be with him even if she found hell as well as heaven in his arms. For the first time in her life she felt desire and it scattered caution to the four winds.

'I think the romantic dreams of girlhood have clung to you rather longer than they cling to others,' he said. 'You have vulnerable wings, my fledgling, and I must take care not to break them.'

She gave a slight shiver and drank quickly from the stemmed glass in her hand. His hands were brown and powerful and alone with him in Fez, and married to him in a country where a wife was a possession, she would be completely at his mercy. She would, in a sense, be a prisoner of his passion to beget a child.

'Your foot swings back and forth like the tail of a nervous cat,' he said. 'You must learn to relax.'

'I—I used to get like this when I had a music examination to pass.' She gave him a nervous smile. 'I was always afraid I'd make a fool of myself and produce awful discordant notes.'

'You are highly strung, *mia lindo*.'

'I'm afraid so, Karim.'

'Don't be afraid.' He raised his glass and swallowed some of his malt whisky. 'I like knowing how sensitive you are.'

Their eyes locked for a long silent moment and Linda felt him consuming her with that look, as if he wanted ownership of her right here on the aircraft.

'Oh, Karim,' her face was nakedly afraid of the emotions he made her feel, 'if only we had more in common!'

'What more could we have?' He spoke indulgently, as if trying to soothe the fears of a child.

'I—I'm so unwordly compared to you—you picked out all my honeymoon clothes because you thought I might have chosen all the wrong things.'

'Linda,' he suddenly looked severe, 'the reason I took you to the salon in Barcelona was simply that I wanted you to have the best. Charming fabrics that truly become you and colours to suit your fair colouring. It pleased me to do the selecting.'

'I feel as if you're buying me, Karim.'

He gave a slight shrug. 'What does it matter, as my wife you must be well dressed and there the matter ends.'

'Spoken just like a bossy Arab with Spanish blood in him!'

'Does the thought of it make you scared?' he mocked.

'I've heard that such men like to keep a woman in her place.'

'They don't just like it, *bint*, they do it,' he said sardonically. 'Spare the rod and spoil the child, as the saying goes—not to mention that a tame husband makes for himself a wild wife.'

'As if any woman could think you tame!' It both troubled and piqued her that there were depths to his nature which she might never explore; always he would want her to be the candid and transparent partner, with an innocent body for his enjoyment, uncheapened by casual affairs.

She met his eyes and saw tiny points of fire in them ... with a look he owned her and it was foolishly romantic of her to want some sign from him that he cared about the person she was inside the young, unfledged body that was to give him a child.

He had seen too much. He had fought in a cruel war and become disillusioned by people and the ideals they talked about and senselessly destroyed. And like most men who survived destruction he wanted to see life renewed in the shape of his own son or daughter.

'Is your desert house very big?' she asked, steering her thoughts into a less disturbing area. 'Your house of the nightingales.'

'It is a fair size,' he replied, 'and jasmine clambers all over the walls and the rooms are filled with the scent of the flower, for the house surrounds a massive courtyard. I have a fondness for it but my castle in Spain was convenient for my work with the loyalist movement. It provided shelter and escape for those like Dona Domaya who needed a place where they could stay for a while and forget what they had been through. Some, like Domaya, will take time to recover ... she refuses, you see, to believe that her husband Luis is dead. Until she can accept the truth she will continue to relive the nightmare.'

He tossed back the remainder of his whisky. 'In Fez you and I will put all our problems behind us and concentrate upon ourselves. *Comprende*?'

She gave him a smile and didn't miss the masterful gleam in his eyes. In Fez they would be cut off from the past and there he would have legal dominion over her future. Her heart beat fast when she thought of what lay ahead of her in the arms of so forceful a man who, unlike herself, was no novice where the pleasures of the body were concerned.

As they ate their delicious lunch Karim told her that he had arranged for their marriage to take place in the main reception room of the house, which had a mosaic floor and a fountain at the centre. He smiled as he described the colonnade set with lotus pools, and the fretted tower which turtle doves had turned into their very own dalliance balcony where they perched and preened their feathers.

It was a house of an almost cloistered beauty and the previous occupiers the nuns had made a garden which he felt certain Linda would find pleasure in. There were blue jacaranda that deepened into exotic shades of mauve in the moonlight, and pink masses of lantana that attracted butterflies with wings as marvellous as jewels. The marigolds of a deep tangerine colour were as big as michaelmas daisies, and on the pools the lotus flowers were ivory white.

Linda ate her gooseberry pie and cream and listened with a touch of fear as Karim described the desert to her. A limitless and pitiless ocean of sand smouldering in the hot sun which as it died at duskfall gave way to masses of diamond bright stars.

'It has a savage fascination.' He stirred brown sugar into his black coffee. 'Even the sea is less awesome than the desert whose storms can stir the sand into huge smoking pillars that speed across its surface like crazed giants. But after such a tempest there is a sense of peace that can't be described. It is empty and infinite . . . the garden of Allah.'

He showed Linda that they were now flying over the desert and she realised that he had left behind in Spain the part of him that was Spanish. As they approached Fez Eldjid she found herself with a man whose Arabian side was now predominant. This was the Sheikh Karim el Khalid, a warlord of this strange and barbaric land whose traditions had undergone far less change than in the Western hemisphere.

This was the land of *mektoub* . . . it is written. The land of the *haram*, that place forbidden to all men but the master of the house. Here in the streets the women still walked veiled, wearing the charms and amulets that kept the eye of Shaitan away from them.

As the aircraft circled for landing Linda accepted that there was no going back to the person she had been . . . she had committed herself to a marriage which in every way would make her the total possession of a man of the East. How long that marriage would last she had no way of knowing . . . perhaps only as long as it took her to give Karim the child he wanted.

The sun shot an arrow of gold through the window beside her seat and it flickered on the surface of the bracelet which Karim had fastened about her wrist. On her other wrist on the much narrower bangle there hung the little heart which enclosed the face of her mother.

As always when Linda felt insecure she found with her fingers that hard little heart. Something caught her by the throat . . . she had never really known what it was like to be loved just for herself. Her mother had walked out on her and her father had handed her over to his sister who had demanded gratitude rather than affection. Even when Aunt Doris had shown any affection it had been of the fretful kind that demanded of a child that she be always neat and respectful and never noisy.

Linda decided then and there that if she had Karim's child and he abided by his promise that she could stay and love it, then never would that child's life be a book of rules. There would be laughter in the playroom, noise and scribbling and cake crumbs over the floor. Don't do this and don't do that would be forbidden words, and when the lightning flashed and the thunder roared that child wouldn't be left to tremble alone under the bedcovers.

'How silent you are.' Large strong hands gripped Linda's and she looked at Karim in a bemused way. 'Are you afraid of coming down to earth?'

'I was thinking of my childhood.' Her eyes dwelt gravely on his face that was so bronzed and so firmly featured. 'If we have a child, Karim, will you let me take care of it?'

'Of course I shall.' He chafed her cold hands in his warm ones. 'I am not so hard hearted that I would separate you from your very own baby.'

'Promise me, Karim.' She was in the grip of a strange anxiety, 'Give me your word!'

'You have my word.' His brows were grooved by a frown. 'What has got into you, Linda? I told you when I proposed to you that I want my child to grow up in the care of its English mother. I chose you deliberately for that purpose. You will be the perfect mother.'

'I shall try to be a good mother,' she said, and foolishly she felt a sting of tears in her eyes. 'I know I shall be a loving one—that's all important, Karim, and I speak from experience. It isn't enough to care about a child's welfare, love and kisses mean such a lot when we're small and can't defend ourselves against adults and the way they can knock down the walls around us.'

'My child, you are quite upset about this.' He gripped her hands and seemed concerned to glimpse tears in her eyes. 'When did I give the impression that I would knock down walls and make you feel insecure all over again?'

She knew the answer . . . it was because he didn't

love her. Quite suddenly, as the aircraft taxied along the private airstrip where they were landing, Linda knew why this feeling of insecurity had her in its grip. But red hot pincers wouldn't have torn the confession from her tongue, that quite unexpectedly she wanted from him the love he had never been able to feel in all his thirty-six years. She wanted to see it in his eyes, wanted to feel it in his touch, wanted to hear it on his lips.

She followed him numbly off the aircraft and into the limousine that waited to take them to the outskirts of Fez where his house was situated on the edge of the desert. She breathed a strange air and was aware of the lofty walls of the city as they drove through the great horseshoe gateway into the heart of the East.

Her own heart was troubled ... she wanted Karim to take her in his arms but such a demonstration in public was forbidden here. This wasn't a European city where couples embraced in the back seats of cars and cabs without any fear of censure. In fact Karim was sitting well away from her on the wide back seat of the limousine, an air of reserve about him that struck at her feelings.

Intent on hiding her feelings Linda gazed intently from the window beside her and saw minarets and domes of a grace that was in contrast to the tumbledown muddle of the streets through which they drove, the blare of the motor horn a constant warning to robed pedestrians and their donkeys.

Poor bedraggled donkeys, over-laden and underfed but still spirited enough to bray back at the car as it passed by in a cloud of dust. Here and there skinny dogs nosed about in alleyways and the figures of dark-clad, robed women were like silent shadows against the sunburned walls of houses which looked a thousand years old. Linda knew they weren't that old but merely unchanged in need and construction.

In a while the old part of the city was left behind and in the rosy decline of the sun Linda saw garden-like terraces and rooftops where the women weren't muffled in robes that concealed them from head to toe. She gazed in fascination at one figure who sat there like a golden statue, the declining sun glinting in the hoops of her earrings, then a child ran to the woman and she stirred out of her trance and drew him close against her.

Linda felt the sensual pulse-beat of this place where time was measured by the calls of the *muezzin*, and when she glanced shyly at Karim, his profile in the deepening golden dusk was pure Arabian. In her mind's eye she visualised him as he would look at their marriage, clad in the robes and insignia of a Sheikh. Then as if feeling her gaze upon him Karim turned his head to look at her and she felt as if she were looking into the fierce eyes of a desert falcon.

'In a day or so we shall visit the bazaars; they are noisy and fascinating.'

'I'd like to do that—it seems a very strange old city.'

'It's the oldest city in Morocco and has remained purely Eastern and timeless. It's my father's birthplace but the old palace in which he was born has long since crumbled into dust.'

She caught the note of sadness in his voice and wanted to reach out and touch his hand in sympathy. Did it mean anything to him that they had both had inwardly lonely childhoods? There was really no telling for he could be so inscrutable, especially right now when he chose to sit so apart from her. It was true what he said, they were strangers until they touched.

Quite suddenly the daylight was gone and a slim moon, like the blade of an Arabian dagger, hung in the sky above the fretted tower which was Linda's first glimpse of the house where she was to become a bride.

When they stepped from the car in the massive courtyard Karim gestured towards the sky. 'See the virgin moon,' he murmured, and the seductive tone of his voice seemed to enfold her as she stood breathing the scent of an unknown flower.

'What is that scent?' she asked and couldn't quite keep a tremor out of her voice.

'The jasmine,' he replied, and as they walked towards a Moorish archway that led into the house she saw masses of the creamy flowers all over the walls, a confusion of them, clinging to the stone and softening its aspect with their starlike florets.

'How lovely!' Linda raised her face to Karim's in the dagger of moonlight and she was unaware that her skin was as luminescent as the jasmine petals.

In a scented silence Karim's hands framed her face and held it upraised to his. 'For our memory book we hold this moment, Linda. It may be that never again will you look so young and unaware, and because of the nature of a man how can I swear that I shall never hurt you?'

'I—I don't expect you to be other than what you are, Karim.' She gazed back into his eyes and spoke the simple truth. From the beginning she had seen temper and danger in his face and she didn't expect the tawny tiger that he was to turn suddenly into a docile tabby cat. It was absurd to think of El Khalid behaving like some of the men she had seen at the country club, allowing themselves to be tethered to wives who seemed to regard marriage as a state of demand and supply.

'You are the most sensitive creature I ever met in my life, Linda. It's your sensitivity which makes such an appeal to what I can only term my toughness, but it can be a dangerous acquisition and you know why.'

'Yes, I know how easily I can be hurt.' It had always been that way and as a child she would agonise for days over the death of a pet, or a harsh word, or something she read in a book. Her teachers called her a dreamer and wrote in her school reports that she didn't always pay attention and lived in a world of her own. Those reports annoyed Aunt Doris but her uncle had understood and that was why he had encouraged her to be a musician.

Karim ran the warm tips of his fingers down the sides of her neck. 'I wonder if you know how much I want you? If by some mischance someone intervened tomorrow and said we couldn't marry, then I'd want to wring his neck with my bare hands.'

'You barbarian,' she exclaimed. 'You make me feel as if I'm going to be owned rather than married.'

He smiled at her remark and didn't attempt to dispute it.

They entered the house which right away captured Linda's imagination and saved her from dwelling on the intimate aspects of her forthcoming marriage. She wanted to be shown the room where the ceremony was to take place and with a smile Karim indulged her. She stood there looking about her ... it was like a room in a palace, she thought, filled with soft lighting and the cool tinkling of water. As she went to approach the fountain her heels clicked upon the mosaic floor and she stood still again and understood why Eastern people wore feltsoled slippers in their houses.

'It's very imposing,' she said softly. 'It makes me feel very English.'

'Such surroundings make you look very English.' He took her by the hand, gripping her fingers possessively. 'Come, there are rooms less formal for you to see and I'm certain you want to bathe and change for supper.'

Oh, such a big house, she thought. Such a strange new life ahead of her!

CHAPTER FIVE

THE *Ras Blanca* was a rambling house and most of the household staff were men clad in snowy white tunics and turbans. The two female members of the staff turned out to be Linda's personal maids and she wondered how on earth she was going to keep them occupied when she was accustomed to taking care of herself. Sofie was to take care of her clothes while Perveneh was to do her hair and help her dress.

There was however, a language problem because neither of them knew a word of English and it wasn't until Sofie started to unpack Linda's luggage that verbal communication was established. Because Linda's clothes were new they were still in the *salon* wrappers and Sofie turned to her excitedly and told her in Spanish that she had relatives in Ibiza and for a while she had worked in their *taberna* and had returned to Fez to be married. At present her husband was doing his National Service and he didn't mind if she worked in a good household while he was away.

'You have a modern minded husband,' Linda smiled.

'In some ways.' Sofie veiled her face with her hand and gave a slight giggle. 'I am pleased to work in this house. The *lellah* has many fine things to wear, and the Sheikh el Khalid is a man very respected and a hero of the war.'

The words sent a shivery thrill through Linda. He would have been much younger at the time and, perhaps, rather more vulnerable than the man he had grown into. War and fighting and other matters he had dealt with had obviously hardened him. 'The Sheikh wishes me to wear Eastern garments for my marriage to him and I'm wondering if you know anything about them, Sofie?'

The Arabian girl gave Linda the conspiratorial look of someone who remembered every detail of her own wedding. 'The orders came a week ago, *lellah*, that I was to do the sewing.' She opened the carved doors of a wardrobe and there hung a dress of palest gold with a diaphanous tunic bordered with tiny pearls. 'Do you like?'

Linda was lost for words as Sofie withdrew the dress on its hanger and showed her how the satin gleamed. 'How clever you are, Sofie,' she said admiringly, though she could see how simply styled the dress was and that it was the satin fabric that made it look so rich.

'Arabian girls learn how to sew when they are very young, *lellah*.' Sofie's doe-shaped eyes glistened from the compliment. 'I sewed all my own wedding garments and all my bed linen and half a dozen shirts for my husband. Is it not the custom in England for a bride to do this?'

'I believe it was many years ago.' Linda stroked her fingertips against the satin in much the same way as Karim had stroked her skin. 'Is there a veil to go with the dress?'

'A veil you must have, *lellah*.' Sofie produced it from the deep drawer of the wardrobe and there seemed to Linda to be yards of it and she just had to laugh.

'The veil is significant,' Sofie said severely. 'The bridegroom is forbidden to look upon your face until you are alone together as man and wife when he is allowed at last to unveil you.'

'I see.' Linda spoke solemnly. 'The bride is gift-wrapped and the bridegroom has the fun of unwrapping her.'

Sofie looked as if she didn't know how to accept Linda's humorous remark, unaware that Linda was making an effort to keep her fears and apprehensions at bay. Though it might be comparatively easy for an Arabian girl to marry a man she barely knew it wasn't so easy for someone as English as Linda. She couldn't help but distrust the feelings she felt when she was with Karim, for up until meeting him she had been more inclined to be excited by a symphonic rhapsody than a man.

Now, though she confessed it only to herself, she felt butterflies inside her at the very thought of being unveiled by Karim.

'I'm very, very pleased with my wedding dress,' she said warmly. 'Were you given instructions to choose that colour?'

Sofie nodded and carefully replaced the dress in the wardrobe. 'His Eminence sent instructions to Husain who runs the household and I was sent to the bazaar to purchase what was required. The satin is of the very best and the gauze tunic and veil were bought ready made, as were the beaded slippers.'

'I had better try those on.' Linda sat down on the long padded stool at the foot of the bed and removed her court shoes. Sofie unwrapped the slippers which were of velvet in a deeper shade of gold with sparkling beads encrusting them. As Linda slid her feet into them she reflected that she was going to look as if she'd stepped out of an illustration for the *Arabian Nights Treasury*, a book she had owned before going to live with Aunt Doris. It had been a present from her mother which she had valued but her aunt had taken it away from her and declared that such stories were a lot of nonsense and in future she was to read the classics. Uncle Henry had an entire set of them bound in deep-red calfskin and they were kept behind the glass doors of a well-polished cabinet. Obedient to a fault Linda had ploughed through *Vanity Fair*, *The Old Curiosity Shop* and *Mill On The Floss*. Oh, what a relief it had been when at last she had been allowed to read Jane Austen's novels.

As the childhood memories filtered through her mind she walked across her bedroom floor in the house where she was going to become a bride and wondered if she could get through the marriage service with pinched toes.

'Your face looks painful, *lellah*.'

'I'm afraid the slippers are too small, Sofie.'

Sofie looked ready to cry but Linda quickly reassured her. She would wear a pair of court shoes and the long skirt of the dress would hide them. 'It wouldn't be fair on the Sheikh,' she smiled, 'if when he unveils me I look as if I'm suffering.'

She removed the slippers with a sigh of relief, and in that instant Perveneh came out of the bathroom and indicated with her slender hands that Linda's bath was ready for her.

There was no privacy any more but as Linda soaked in the subtle herbal essences she decided to endure the company of these two Arabian girls. They were gentle and friendly and she didn't want them to lose their jobs just because she was shy about being seen in the nude.

They flitted about her while she dressed for dinner in a turquoise dress of softest shantung; it had lovely flowing lines and the full sleeves fell open at the elbow, making her feel cool and at ease. Her hair was brushed until it shone and Perveneh invited her to sniff the perfume in a globe-shaped bottle which had a little glass wand attached to the stopper.

It was faintly musky but rather nice and Linda applied some with the little wand to the backs of her earlobes. Almost instantly, as her skin warmed the perfume, it floated around her in a fragrant wave and she realised that it was an authentic Arabian scent and far less subtle than the delicate kind she usually wore.

Oh well, if she was going to be the bride of an authentic Sheikh then she might as well enjoy the role. In her turquoise shantung and her scent she floated along the colonnade where the ivory-white lotus flowers spun on the pools set into the marble floor. Darting gold fish spun the flowers for a boy dressed all in white was feeding them tiny pellets of food. He glanced up shyly at Linda and regarded her with sloping dark eyes but when she smiled at him, he quickly lowered his gaze and went on feeding the fish.

Two white-robed attendants stood at the entrance of the *sala* where Karim awaited her clad in a white dinner-jacket, a plain white shirt and matt-black trousers. His black eyebrows slowly elevated as he took in her appearance. He came towards her in a deliberate way and without saying a word he took both of her hands into his and carried them to his lips where he kissed the insides of her wrists. With his look and with that light brush of his lips he seemed to touch the sensual centre of her being. It seemed as if everything she had ever felt in her life was intensified by this moment . . . it was as if all her life rushed past her and then found its terminus in the commanding figure of the Sheikh Karim el Khalid.

'I was right to bring you here,' he said. 'You light up my desert house and seem to belong here and I look in your eyes and they are no longer the eyes of an anxious child in a strange new world. You like this place, eh?'

'I feel,' her smile was tremulous, 'as if I've stepped into the *Arabian Nights Treasury*. It was a book I once had and it was all about Haroun al Raschid who was a prince with magic powers.'

'And do you think I have magic powers?' Karim smiled.

'Of a kind.' She gazed back at him and despite his modern suit he was very much a part of the oriental strangeness of this room; its dusky corners, rich drapery and brass-chained lamps hanging from the carved ceiling where sculpted falcons and ibises flew across the panels in perfect detail.

'Then allow me to perform a sleight of hand.' From his pocket he took something that glistened and stepping behind her, where she felt him disturbingly close to her, he fastened a long chain of diamonds about her neck. 'These are moon diamonds because they are found in the desert by the light of the moon.'

Linda couldn't believe the beauty of the gems shining around her like tiny-spoked wheels of fire. 'Y-you are so generous, Karim.'

'Because you will be generous in return.' His hands closed warm and strong on her waist, his fingers pressing through the shantung of her dress to imprint themselves upon her body. 'You will give me yourself and what diamond can compare to the jewel of innocence?'

She felt a kind of delicious terror at his words. Her knees went boneless and she couldn't utter a sound as he turned her slowly around in his hands as if to admire his new possession from every angle.

'You wear a very provocative perfume,' he murmured, his eyes looking directly into hers. 'Wear it tomorrow.'

Linda smiled nervously. 'I think it's the kind that clings for a week.'

'And will you be the kind who clings for a week?'

'I expect I will be if I don't get something to eat.'

'Ah, then let us have supper for I don't want a faint-hearted bride.' He led her to the divan where the table was laid and there they ate their *cous-cous*, the first that Linda had ever tasted and succulent with lamb, vegetables, rice and herbs. She was ravenous even if she did look ethereal in the turquoise dress and the moonstones, and it was also intimate to be eating from the same dish as Karim.

'Good?' He regarded her with an amused glint in his eyes.

'Mmm, I just can't help gorging myself.'

'I like to see a healthy appetite.'

'I've heard that men of the East like women to be plump.'

'Ah, that was in the old days when women were expected to be indolent inmates of the *haram*, but here at the *Ras Blanca* there is a swimming pool and a tennis court and a stable of Berber horses. If you aren't a horsewoman then I shall teach you.'

'You will have to, Karim.' She drank some of the light wine served with their meal. 'All my spare time was given to my music.'

'I hope you don't miss your music too much?'

'I do have stabs of conscience about it because I used to practice every day.'

'It was quite a taskmaster, eh?'

She nodded and when she gave him a rather uncertain look he leaned forward and kissed her mouth. 'Don't look like that, child, as if you think I am going to be a taskmaster. I suggest that you learn to ride because riding in the desert can be a great pleasure and you and I must share all the pleasures.'

Her heart beat tumultuously when he said that and she was unaware that her hand gripped the diamond chain which he had hung about her neck. He was generous, courteous and impeccably groomed yet none of it could hide his essential untamed look. When she pleased him, he gave her things but something warned Linda that there was a side to him that was relentless as the desert itself and there was no way she could be his wife and not encounter the dark side of him as well as the light.

'I know what is going through your mind, Linda.'

'Do you?' Her eyes dwelt gravely on his face.

'You feel a mixture of doubts and fears, my sweet, but there is a certain feeling you can't fight.'

'A-and what is that?'

'Desire.' He breathed it warmly against her lips. 'The desire you and I will share ... it will be the mainspring of the marriage we make tomorrow for be in no doubt that your cool sweetness of face and body are very pleasing to me. You will learn in my arms what you are made for.'

After coffee he swung a cashmere cloak around her shoulders and they took a walk around the great courtyard where the moonlight shimmered on the jasmine and a soft breeze stirred the nectar cups of the laburnum trees. Attached to the stone walls were lamps in fretwork and beyond those walls the desert sprawled and the spaciousness of it was both fascinating and fearful to Linda. Overhead the stars seemed close and silvery and the pulsating croak of cicadas filled the night.

Karim talked of the desert which he had known and explored since a boy, and then all at once a savage, drawn-out growl echoed beyond the boundary walls of *Ras Blanca* and Linda found herself clutching Karim's arm.

'Only a sandcat,' he drew her hand into the warmth of his. 'They are rather menacing and have a habit of creeping into courtyards at night in search of water. All part of the desert.'

He spoke with such equanimity and when Linda glanced up at him, his face in the moonlight had a haunting quality, a hint of the sinister where shadow lurked beneath the facial bones. For her Karim was like the desert, he held all the allure and danger of the unknown and tomorrow she would belong to him absolutely.

Her gaze slid down the lean hardness of his profile to the wide stretch of his shoulders, and her body felt alive with a complexity of feelings. For a heart, she wondered, did he have a desert stone? He had hinted as much and Linda believed him entirely when he asserted that love meant nothing to him.

Love was too tenuous an emotion for someone so strong . . . instead he substituted a sense of possession where she was concerned. A proud, tempered, fatalistic man . . . his own master and hers!

'I wonder,' his eyes gazed down into hers, 'are you a romantic who has dreamed of a love that even death can't destroy?'

'If I were that kind of dreamer I would hardly be here with you,' she replied.

'True, *mia lindo*, and now I must allow you to go to your bed for tomorrow we face a big day in our lives.

You look composed but I wonder . . .' He slid a hand inside the cloak and laid it against her heart and as always when he touched her, her sensory reaction was dramatic. She heard him catch his breath, then he gathered her close to him and kissed her for a long time, in a pulsating silence that drove their bodies desperately together.

They finally went indoors and parted from each other. They wouldn't meet again until they stood in front of the Ma'zoun and made their vows.

'Good night,' he cradled her hands against his lips, 'and sweet dreams.'

'Good night, Karim.' She drifted away from him and when she reached the end of the colonnade she glanced back for a fleeting moment and he was still there, leaning against one of the palm-shaped columns, carrying a flame to a cigar. Tomorrow they wouldn't part to go their separate ways to bed . . . tomorrow Karim el Khalid would be her husband and as if tiny wings of panic attached themselves to her heels Linda fled into her bedroom, startled and concerned to find Perveneh half-asleep on the stool at the foot of the bed.

Linda went across to the young maid and drew her to her feet. As best she could she indicated that Perveneh was to go to her own bed and not wait up for her. The girl shook her head and looked a little frightened, as if she had been given orders by Husain to always be on hand to assist the *lellah* with her toilette.

Tomorrow, Linda decided, she would ask Sofie to tell Pervenah not to wait up for her. She was only about sixteen and even though she persisted in helping Linda to prepare for bed she couldn't stop herself from yawning.

'Go to bed!' With a slight laugh Linda drew the girl to the door and shooed her away. '*Emshi besselema.*'

The girl broke into a smile that revealed her pearly teeth. '*Leyltak sayeedah, lellah.*'

Alone at last, Linda slid beneath the gauzy pavilion around her bed and settled down against the soft pillows with a sigh of relief. She felt tired but she knew that sleep was going to be elusive; so many thoughts were milling about in her mind and she also felt a vagrant sense of guilt because she was going to be married and her aunt and uncle wouldn't be present.

They had raised her and she had always been particularly fond of Uncle Henry. He would have liked to be the one who gave her away on her wedding day, she knew that. How would he feel when he and Aunt Doris received her letter and learned that she had become the wife of a man who was part Arab.

Aunt Doris had talked of Spaniards as if they were half-civilised so she was bound to get into one of her states when she read Linda's letter.

By the time it arrived on the doormat in the well-polished hall of the mock-Tudor house Linda would be well and truly the wife of the Sheikh Karim el Khalid and the very thought was enough to quicken her pulse rate. She wouldn't lie alone in bed tomorrow night ... she would be in his strong brown arms, learning all the secrets that all down the years had driven men and women to seek each other.

Each so different, with ideals and dreams as opposite as their physical beings. How could a man not have a strong, logical outlook on the world when he was equipped with a muscular body made to thrust its way through life and to take on burdens? How could a woman not be the prey of man when the very

shape of her invited all that was predatory in the male
of the species?

The cello and the bow, she thought, making the
divinest music in the world ... or the most
disharmonious of sounds.

Her fingers gripped the *broderie Arabe* that edged
the big soft pillows and a medley of emotions swept
her body. Each tick of the clock brought her nearer to
the moment when she pledged herself to Karim.
Desire, he had said, was to be the mainspring of their
marriage and instinctively she knew that when desire
lost its lustre there might be nothing left but a look of
disinterest in his eyes. The flame that had burned in
them while they stood together in the courtyard might
be quenched and Linda lay in the big carved bed in
this big strange room and yearned for the wisdom of a
mother who would soothe her anxieties.

Her fingers sought the little heart on the schoolgirl
bracelet that still fitted her slender wrist. The one
memento of her mother which Aunt Doris had not
succeeded in taking away from her. She had tried, of
course, but the tiny latch on the bracelet would never
yield and this enabled Linda to wear it night and day.

Tonight it was her only link with the mother whose
whereabouts were unknown to her. If Miriam was still
with her American musician then she was probably
somewhere in the States, and Linda thought of those
times when she had felt like tracing her mother. But a
certain shyness held her back, along with a hurt
feeling that never really went away. How could a
woman abandon her very own child; and that thought
inevitably led her back to why Karim was marrying
her at midday tomorrow in the mosaic room where the
fountain played. That cool sound would be their
wedding music, and in an effort to be calm Linda

focused her thoughts on her wedding dress and what pair of shoes to wear with it.

A pity about the beaded slippers ... they danced golden and glittering ahead of her, leading her into the realms of sleep. She lay curled on her side, her left arm flung across the pillow, her slim fingers still gripping the *broderie Arabe*, unaware when a brown hand drew aside the netting and dark eyes studied her sleeping form in the shaft of light from the colonnade beyond her room.

The light set gleaming the little heart on her bracelet, and when she gave a sudden restless shift in her sleep the netting fell softly back into place and a moment later the room was dark again.

Linda awoke to see rays of sunlight dancing through the fretwork of the window screens. She gave a lazy stretch and looked around her, finding herself in a room like no other she had ever slept in ... exotic with its deep oriental carpets, ivory-white walls and dark furniture with intricate carvings all over it. There was a chest with numerous painted drawers, a hoarder's paradise.

She was returning from the bathroom when Perveneh entered the bedroom carrying a breakfast tray. She dipped into a curtsey, and with a good morning smile Linda indicated that Perveneh set down the tray on the rosewood table that stood in front of the window divan. Beyond those windows the sun was shining across the tawny spaciousness of the desert and Linda had the feeling that Karim was out there, in the saddle of one of his Berber horses and untroubled by the nervous fears his bride-to-be was feeling.

Her breakfast tray looked inviting and Linda found

that after she had finished her orange juice she felt ready for the deliciously crisp rolls and honey and, as always, the coffee was a joy. She could feel Perveneh and Sofie watching her as they went about their tasks and she smiled to herself. This was her wedding morning and they were probably wondering why she appeared so calm . . . an air of calm that was all on the surface.

Linda dallied at the table, reluctant to place herself in the hands of her maids until it was necessary. The sands of her single days were running out and for a little while longer she wanted to think of herself as Linda Layne. She wondered in a casual way what Larry Nevins and other members of the country club would say when the word got around that she had become a Sheikha. That would be her official title as the wife of Karim and it was so unbelievably exotic that it was bound to cause a few shock waves.

'She takes after her mother,' friends of Aunt Doris would say.

Was it true? Linda poured herself another cup of coffee and decided that it probably was. She had her mother's musical inclinations so it wasn't too surprising if she had the other traits that made her mother reject the conventional pathways.

Only now did she fully realise that she herself had also rejected them. The rejection had begun when she answered the advertisement in *The Lady* and sought employment that would take her away from the neatly ordered lives of her aunt and uncle and their coterie of friends.

'The time ticks by, *lellah*.' The slightly anxious voice of Sofie broke in on her thoughts. 'There is much to be done to prepare you for your marriage.'

'My marriage,' Linda echoed. 'It really is going to take place, isn't it? I'm not just dreaming.'

Sofie shook her head in its light covering of silk and her eyes scanned Linda's face. 'You are happy, *lellah*?'

'Of course,' Linda replied, but it wasn't quite true. What she felt was a tingling sense of expectancy, as if she were going to the theatre where an unusual play was to take place. That play would be dramatic and exciting, but was it designed for happiness?

Ravishing scents were stealing out from the bathroom and Linda submitted to the attentions of her maids. While she soaked in the water Perveneh manicured her fingernails and varnished them a soft rose colour and when she stepped from that Byzantine bath a rosescented lotion was massaged into her skin. During this process Perveneh said something to Sofie that made her giggle.

'Do share the joke,' Linda said, and she was past the stage of feeling embarrassed by all these attentions to her body . . . the pale, precious body that on the stroke of noon would become the property of the Sheikh.

Sofie put her lips to Linda's ear and whispered that unlike women of the East she had not had the golden hair removed from her secret areas. It was the custom and they could provide her with a razor if she wished.

Although Linda laughed she also blushed for she had been reared by an aunt who had disliked references to the body and the part it played in the scheme of things. When Linda was thirteen she had been expected to know about a certain traumatic happening without being told; she had known from the girls at school but all the same it had been a bit of a shock but Aunt Doris had offered not a jot of comfort and endearingly it had been Uncle Henry who had come quietly upstairs with a cup of tea and talked to Linda about the whimsies of nature.

'The Sheikh knows he's marrying an English bride, Sofie. He won't expect me to—conform.'

A little later, scented like a rose, Linda was ceremoniously clad in a sheer silk slip which was her only garment beneath the glimmering satin of her wedding dress, and now she understood why Sofie had been upset because the beaded slippers were too small. They were meant for bare feet, whereas a pair of court shoes looked clumsy unless worn with the sheerest of tights.

Perveneh and Sofie started to argue and Linda kept hearing the word *babouches*, the Arabian word for slippers, and she was about to suggest that she hobble to her marriage in the beaded gold slippers that made her feel desperately sorry for Chinese women who used to have their feet bound when Perveneh darted out of the room.

'What on earth is wrong?' Linda wanted to know.

'She has a pair of *babouches* she has never worn and they might fit the *lellah*.'

'That's kind of Perveneh. I'd like you to tell her, Sofie, not to wait up for me at night. The poor child was falling off to sleep when I came to bed last night.'

'Child?' Sofie looked mystified. 'She isn't a child, *lellah*.'

'But Perveneh can't be more than sixteen.'

'No, but she is not a child. Arabian girls start early to be women, *lellah*, and it is her duty to wait upon you and she would be upset and afraid of the Sheikh's anger if she failed to be on hand when you come to your bed.'

'I see.' Linda stood there in the golden dress and contrasted the pampered lives of English girls with those of Sofie and Perveneh who were so willing and good humoured and both so strikingly pretty with their *café au lait* skins and huge, long-lashed eyes. If they were to appear in white tennis dresses on the courts of the Kingswood Country Club they'd be besieged by the young men who played there.

Perveneh came running back into the bedroom clutching a package to her chest. When unwrapped it contained a pair of dove-soft blue slippers with wedge heels, and there were sighs of relief when Linda slid her toes into them and they clasped her feet as if made for her.

'I've something old,' Linda touched her bracelet with the heart attached, 'and I've something blue. My dress is new and to complete the rhyme I must borrow from you, Sofie.'

'It is English superstition?' Sofie asked.

'A very old one.'

'A *feisha* to turn away the evil eye?' Sofie looked intrigued by the idea that English women could also be aware of the dark powers.

'Yes, something like that.'

'Then I would like the *lellah* to wear one of my amulets.' Sofie removed one of the chains that hung about her neck and showed Linda the charm which was attached to it, a little capsule carved in ivory which contained a Koranic prayer.

'Thank you, Sofie.' The amulet hung round her neck with Karim's chain of diamonds, then the diaphanous tunic was slipped over her head and the mirror on the wall showed her that she was halfway to looking like an Arabian bride. Next came the finishing touches and after the *kohl* was applied to her eyelids with a soft feather she stared in wonderment at herself. The cosmetic had somehow turned her eyes to gold, and Perveneh's clever fingers did something to her hair that made the ends turn softly upwards, creating a subtle difference ... a kind of sensuous glamour, Linda realised.

Midway through these ministrations there was a discreet knock on the bedroom door and Sofie returned from opening it with a little jewel box of white kidskin. Linda wasn't surprised by what the box contained, it was the anklet which Karim had asked her to wear only it wasn't the simple chain he had indicated. It was fashioned of tiny golden hearts all linked together and wearing it gave Linda a sensuous feeling at the pit of her stomach.

'Oh God,' she exclaimed, 'I look like an odalisque!' She wanted to take everything off and wear the simplest garment in her wardrobe but time had run out and she had to face Karim in all this exotic finery.

Sofie stood ready with the wedding *hezaam*, the veil that covered her from head to heel. Linda couldn't have said what her feelings were as she was led along the colonnade of lotus pools to the room where a group of men awaited her, foremost among them her bridegroom impeccably robed in sombre blue, his headcloth bound with golden ropes.

Her heart pounded as he came towards her with an air of easy grace in the Arabian robes that turned him into someone she hardly knew. His face in the frame of the headcloth was bronzed and rather severe and when he reached her, he stood gazing at her from lidded eyes as if he were appraising a canvas.

She certainly felt unreal, the veiling of flowered lace making her feel like a quail in the net, as El Khalid had termed it.

He took her by the hand and led her across the beautifully tiled floor to where the Ma'zoun stood on a silky prayer mat waiting to conduct the marriage service. But first he spoke to them, pausing between sentences so Karim could translate his words to Linda. He spoke of the cultural and religious differences between the East and the West but said that marriage between a man and a woman was based on the same principles all over the world. That the couple should abide in peace and passion and always have respect for each other.

Linda stood there in a kind of dream as she was married to the Sheikh Karim el Khalid de Torres, their hands being bound by Meccan green silk as Karim pledged to take her under his care and protection, the pledging and the binding being duly done in the presence of their witnesses. A legal document in Arabic was then produced and they both had to sign it, the pen unsteady in her own hand though Karim's signature was firm and bold.

Karim didn't take her into his arms and kiss her as was the custom in the West. She was securely veiled except for the silk-edged slits that enabled her arms to be free, and she was aware that men of the East refrained from touching their wives in public. A wife was a man's very private affair and today El Khalid looked like his father's people; he had a lordly air that was enhanced by his Arab clothing.

Now the marriage service was over Linda was led away to the *sala* where the evening before she had enjoyed supper with Karim. Today her husband would remain with his male friends for an hour or so and she would be left to eat alone. She didn't mind in the least because she needed time in which to adjust to the strangeness of finding herself married, especially to a man of such a different background.

Cool lemonade was brought to her in a glass which

stood in a silver, filigreed container. She drank it
thirstily and leaned back against a cushion, glad to be
free of the bridal veil for a while. A light meal was
served on the divan table, consisting of a fluffy
omelette to which a delicious cheese sauce had been
added, then crescent-shaped almond cakes were served
with refreshing mint tea.

When the table was cleared Linda relaxed in the
serene beauty of the *sala* with its fascinating tilework
in a design of golden birds.

So now she was a Sheikha and no longer a part of
the life she had left behind in England. Although a few
minor concessions had been made at the marriage
because she was English she was in no doubt that
where a woman was concerned Karim was entirely an
Arab. She now belonged exclusively to him and her
interests and ideals must fit in with his.

When in a while he came to her, he would be lord of
her body and master of her fate.

CHAPTER SIX

For a moment Linda felt herself go weak and she clung to Karim's arm. The feel of him was real enough; she actually was the bride of this lordly person who came at last to claim her in the veiling she had replaced when Husain came hurriedly to tell her that his Eminence was bidding farewell to his friends.

They walked side by side along the colonnade and this time they passed her bedroom and were heading for his apartment. Linda felt him looking down at her but she just couldn't bring herself to meet his eyes; she heard him laugh softly as if, for now, her shyness was acceptable to him.

When they reached the arched door that led into the master suite Karim suddenly spoke. 'It's the custom, is it not, for a husband to carry his bride across the threshold of their bedroom?'

And before she could even think of a reply he swept her up into his arms, a flare to his nostrils and a glint of possessiveness in his eyes as he carried her through the archways into a room dominated by a king-sized bed.

'Do you know how this custom arose?' He stood there holding her in his arms and his insistent gaze drew her eyes to his face. 'It stems from the rape of the Sabine women, when the Roman centurions rode through their village, snatched them from their homes and made off with them weeping and pleading. Perhaps not a very romantic thing to do at the time but the passage of the years has turned it into a legend. You, Linda, are my Sabine bride whom I have snatched from your pursuits and carried off.'

'I—I'm not complaining.' She spoke more bravely than she felt now she found herself so entirely alone with him.

'Complaints would fall upon deaf ears if you did.' His arms left their strong impression upon her as he lowered her to her feet and scanned her through her bridal veiling. He looked immeasurably tall and dark in this room where they were shut away from the rest of the world ... a spacious bedoom of oriental splendour.

'Everything is like a dream,' she murmured.

'Shall I pinch you awake?' His thick lashes only partly screened the look which told her she belonged to him and he had every right to do with her whatever he wished.

Linda studied his face and still that look was there and would always be there, distinction at war with a ruthlessness which his Arab clothing brought into prominence. She had bound herself to him and must accept the consequences.

'How distinguished you are in your robes, Karim.' She was struck by a combination of feelings for this man whose experiences differed so widely from her own. The very look of him could make her feel shy let alone the fact that she was his bride.

'I can barely see you, my child, for all this veiling which cocoons you.' With firm brown hands he started to unveil her and Linda felt his sense of possession when his fingers came into contact with her satin-clad body. Directly she was free of the veil his hands moved caressingly up and down her spine and his lips left a trail of heat across her throat where they paused to savour the fluttering of her pulse beneath her soft, rose-scented skin.

As her breath quickened his lips slid warm into the contour of her shoulder and she heard him pull air into his nostrils, as if he were breathing her in. She sensed how it aroused him that she had never been with a man; that she was totally untaught in the ways of a man with a woman.

'It almost seems a sin that you must lose your shyness,' he murmured. 'You are shy of me, aren't you, Linda?'

'I can't help myself.' She pressed her face into his robes. 'You are that sort of a man.'

'And you are a girl I would have no different from head to heel.' His hand stroked down over her hair and face, down over her neck to her breast where his fingers gathered hold of the diaphanous tunic and pulled her free of it. Watching her face he traced the contours of her breasts through the satin of her wedding dress, then his fingers wandered round behind her where a row of satin-covered buttons sealed her in to the hips.

Linda's heart started to pound as she felt his fingers undoing the buttons of her dress, exposing the pale shoulders in the slip of water-lily silk. Her body tingled at the brush of his fingertips and a blush ran all over her as she met his gaze, slumberously burning in the shadow of his black lashes.

Slowly he undressed her and dropped her garments to the floor. 'I have wanted to do this ever since the day we met.' He ran his warm hands all over her and she quivered at his touch. He lifted her and laid her on the bed and she watched in helpless anticipation as he rapidly disrobed, disclosing the brown-skinned power of his body and the iron-hard strength of his legs.

He held Linda's gaze with his as he leaned over her creamy nakedness, then slowly his lips travelled downward, lingering on the pink-tipped swell of her breasts, the smooth slope of her hips and the shadowy navel just above her golden mound of Venus. Though Linda felt a certain trepidation it was exciting and she breathed Karim's warmth as he came closer and fondled where his lips had explored.

The lids of Linda's eyes had a languorous feeling as arousal began to pulse its way through her body and limbs. It was as if nothing existed outside this room where she lay in the lacelike patterns thrown through the window screens by the afternoon sun. Her limbs obeyed age-old instincts and her fingers gripped the thick silk on which she lay and her slim vibrating body was as exciting to herself as it was to Karim.

She sensed that for a while he didn't wish her to touch him and she was submissive to his desires, his dominance, and her golden head gave a luxurious toss from side to side as his touch induced in her a sensation that shot golden fire through her system.

'Oh, yes.' Her delight filled her eyes as his lips teased back and forth. 'Oh, Karim—darling!'

'What a surprise you are.' He breathed the words against her skin. 'Your sweet, deceptive coolness is melting like ice in the hot sun and you are even more responsive than I dreamed you would be—I could almost believe that you have Latin blood in your veins.'

'No,' she smiled into his dark and fascinating eyes, 'I haven't any Latin blood but I——'

But he wasn't listening to her and the moment his mouth descended their lips clung hotly, their breath mingled, and when it started to hurt Linda's fingernails dug into his shoulders until his persistence made her gasp his name . . . gasp as if she were going to drown.

She lay there in his strong arms, lips parted, little panting breaths escaping her as his hands gathered her right into him, there at the small of her back as he drove the pleasure right through the yielding arch of her body, deep into the welcoming centre of her where the pain disintegrated.

For endless moments Linda was engulfed in the sensations that swept her mind right out of her body. Her only coherence was his name spilling from her lips as she felt the powerful surges of his passion. Sometimes the pleasure seemed everywhere, and then it would find a core of concentration that lifted her into a rapturous pliable arc, her slim neck reclining backwards until her golden hair brushed the pillows.

What Linda hadn't dreamed was that it could be such wondrous fun as well as pleasure, the laughter intensifying the joy. The glow of the sun gradually declined to hammered bronze, then shadowed mauve shifted into a velvety pall of darkness. The lamp was on when Linda became aware of Karim looking at her. He smiled, then leaning over he buried his lips in her soft hollows, tracing with tonguetip the quivering nerves beneath the smoothness of her stomach.

'I think already that it has happened.'

'What has?' she whispered.

'I have got you with child.'

'It would be a miracle, Karim, if you hadn't.'

He laughed softly and trailed a kiss from breast to breast. 'In certain ways you are still quite a child yourself but I am a selfish, arrogant male, *mia farah*, and from such hours as we have enjoyed an extraordinary child must come. It was enjoyment for you after those first moments?'

'Yes.' She barely breathed the word for still he made her shy despite the hours of intimacy, and her toes curled into the disordered silk of the bedcover as he stroked upwards from her feet, along the slimness of her legs, into those sensitive realms where the merest brush of a fingertip made her open her lips for his kisses.

Her body yielded itself to him and the sweet, wanton wildness that she felt was beyond anything she had dreamed. Like other girls she had been curious and sometimes she had wondered what all the fuss was about, but now she had the answer in the powerful arms of this man who seemed intent on savouring every part of her.

This marvellous male body made her pulsate with exquisite, shuddering pleasure. As from a distance she heard her own voice saying indistinguishable things and the feeling which filled her was so heavenly that she wanted it never to end. She clung to the strong shoulders and rode with him through the spaces of the night where points of fire shot their glowing heat through flesh and bone. They were locked, one into the other in plunging, breathless rapture, and at last her tired hands slid down the wet slopes of his back as she drifted back to awareness ... her eyes gradually opened and she languidly raised a hand to wipe away droplets of sweat from his face.

'Oh, Karim,' she moved against him in the voluptuous aftermath of her pleasure.

'Oh, Linda.' He gazed downward into her pleasured eyes, his chest hair matted and wet. 'That was an incredible joy ride, *mia*, and you are a very passionate young woman, do you know that?'

'I do now,' she smiled, pressing a hand to his chest so she could savour the pounding of his heart. 'Are you pleased with me, lord of my body and master of my fate?'

'Intensely delighted, *arousa*.'

'Is that an Arabian word?'

'It means bride or doll.' He rolled to one side and drew her into the warm brown circle of his arm, and they lay together in the stillness and sweet slackness of spent passion, adrift in their various thoughts. The after-throbs within Linda were deliciously persistent, and turning her head she kissed Karim on the salty shoulder.

'I'm not a bit sorry now that I married you,' she said.

'You look so demure lying beside me but that look is so deceiving it is hardly credible.' Smiling to himself he fingered the slim, schoolgirl bracelet that encircled her left wrist. He drew her wrist forward into the lamplight and studied the little heart inscribed with her mother's name.

'Miriam?' Karim's gaze lifted from the heart to Linda's face, his dark eyes narrowing thoughtfully. 'Is that an English name?'

'No,' Linda smiled and stroked her palm across his chest so the dark hair tickled her skin, 'it's Judaic. My mother's relations were almost wiped out by the Nazis, only her father survived by escaping from a labour camp in Holland where he joined a resistance movement. When the war ended he came to England and opened a little hardware shop, then he married and my mother was born.'

Linda wore a soft little smile as she spoke, but her smile began to fade as she noticed the rather grim set to Karim's mouth and jaw. He released the little heart and let it fall back against her wrist where it rested warm from his hand. He raised himself and drew away from her . . . the pleasure had given way in his eyes to a cold look.

'Why did you never speak of your mother before?' There was an edge to his voice, and the muscles of his chest and shoulders were tautly outlined in the lamplight. Gone entirely was his look of sensual relaxation after their lovemaking.

Perplexed by his manner Linda stared at him and for some reason she found herself tugging the sheet over her exposed breasts. 'I don't talk a lot about her because—well, she walked out on my father when I was only a child and that's why I went to live with my aunt and uncle. I—I never see her. I don't even know if she's still alive.'

'Why did you never mention your mother's background?' He scowled as he spoke and Linda's fingers clenched the sheet that covered her body . . . the body that still pulsated from his passionate attentions.

'Why are you so angry, Karim?' She felt bewildered by him and suddenly afraid . . . it was as if her lover had turned into a forbidding stranger. 'What have I done?'

'As if you didn't know, Linda!'

'I don't know—believe me.'

'I am an Arab on my father's side!' He struck a hand against his chest. 'How do I justify to myself and my compatriots a wife who is related to those who were part of the fighting in which my father was brutally killed? The attack that so injured my mother in her mind that she lost the will to survive my father—you tell me how I justify that!'

His words struck through Linda like a knife and she felt a wave of faintness that washed all the colour out of her face and left her eyes startling in their jewel-like clarity.

'Oh—Karim.' She crouched away from him and searched his face which looked so fierce and proud . . . so Arabian. She hadn't given it a thought that he might have such a fearful reason for hating her mother's people. Despite Miriam's abandonment of her Linda still loved her . . . just as Karim still revered the memory of his parents.

Linda shuddered coldly as the warm remnants of passion drained out of her body. 'Does it have to matter so much?' Her voice was barely above a whisper. 'Nobody knows outside this room——'

'I know, you little fool!' Karim leapt from the bed with the anger of a man who felt himself betrayed. 'This is a serious matter and it should have been discussed between us—you led me to believe your mother was of the Christian faith.'

'Y-you never asked——' Tears welled into Linda's eyes, aroused by a combination of emotions. 'You took everything for granted—even that I'd marry you. You know you did!'

'There would have been no marriage had I known about *this*.' He leaned down to hook a finger in the wristlet, holding it so the links bit into her flesh. 'When I told you that my father was killed?'

'You never told me.' She shook her head at him, tears spilling on to her face. 'It was Adoracion who told me how your parents died but she never said anything about the people responsible. How was I to know . . .?'

He stared down at her distressed face, then let go of her wristlet and turned his back on her. She gazed at his strong, splendid body and couldn't forget how she had lain in his arms for pleasure filled hours, now her enraptured feelings felt lacerated by the furious change in him.

It didn't seem possible that they could have been so close, and now were pushed apart by the enmity that raged back and forth across the desert sands, erupting every so often into fierce clashes of temperament and ideals at cross purposes. People got caught in the middle of those outbursts and it had happened to Karim's eminent father and the mother who had never recovered from the shock of seeing her husband battered to death. Linda's heart ached for Karim, and for herself.

'Don't push me away from you,' she pleaded. 'I—I never meant to cause any harm—I'd sooner die than have you hate me!'

For endless moments he didn't speak, then he turned to confront her, reaching at the same time for his discarded robe. He shrugged into it and all the time his eyes were raking over her . . . with her tousled gold hair and smudged eyes she looked very young and troubled.

'Hate is an evocative word, Linda,' he said at last. 'Hate has a habit of planting its seed deep inside us.'

'W-what are you going to do?' She brushed away her tears with her hand, rather like a forlorn child. 'Do you want me to go——?'

'Don't talk childish nonsense.' He thrust his hands deep into the pockets of his robe. 'I can't decide for the moment what to do, I shall have to give it some thought.'

'Oh, Karim, are you going to let something I can't help come between us?' She kneeled upon the bed and the sheet slid away from her body, baring her breasts. 'I've given myself to you and now you want to throw me away.'

Her words touched him for a spasm of regret crossed his proud Arab features. Their eyes clung and for long silent moments they shared images and emotions too potent to be easily erased from their senses.

'I wish,' he said at last, 'that I had looked at that engraved heart before I took your virginity, but we have been intimate and there is every chance that I have given you a child. In that case we shall have to wait and see what occurs. If you become pregnant then I can't dismiss you from my life. I can't be that cruel to you.'

'And what happens if we haven't made a baby?' Linda felt as if she might suffocate from the mad beating of her heart; as it was she was shaking from head to heel.

'Then it is over,' he said tonelessly.

'Just like that, Karim?' Her voice trembled with the trembling of her body. 'After you insisted—after you made me marry you?'

'Kismet is not always kind,' he rejoined, his face as if carved from desert stone. 'Kismet is sometimes cruel.'

'It's you who are cruel—you!' Suddenly Linda felt driven to express her pain and disregarding her nakedness she leapt from the bed and raising her hand she struck him across his stony face, again and yet again.

The sounds of the slaps and the stinging sensation in her fingers brought Linda back to her senses. She reeled away from him, her eyes almost prenaturally aglow in her white face. Shadows had appeared beneath her eyes and she looked as if she had just been tortured.

'I'm not sorry for hitting you,' she breathed. 'All along my instinct warned me against you a-and when we were in Barcelona I should have gone running to the British consulate and they'd have assisted me in getting home to England. Oh God, how I want to be there right now—now that I've tainted you with my touch. What a pity we don't live in the days when Arab lords could dispose of a woman by having her sold into slavery.'

'Listen to me, you little fool,' his iron jaw didn't show the marks of her fingers but his eyes were smouldering with anger, 'even in this day and age I could very easily do what you have just suggested.'

'Why not?' She shrugged her bare shoulders and had almost forgotten that she confronted him without a stitch on her body. 'I'm sure I could quite easily vanish from your desert house—your naïve British bride who wandered off among the sand dunes and perhaps got herself eaten by the jackals.'

'Enough of that!' His voice whipped at her and made her flinch ... was it only a dream, all that possessive passion of his embrace, all that cradling comfort when they had lain entwined in the great bed? Had they really been lovers who had wanted never to come apart? The only reality now was that they faced each other across a gulf filled with his hatred of the people who had killed his father.

Linda gazed at Karim in the forlorn hope of seeing some reminder of the man who had taken her for his own and made it seem like heaven on earth.

But no, when she looked into his eyes she saw an unrelenting stranger gazing back at her. Feeling lost and desperately hurt she turned away from him and crouched down on the foot of the bed, huddling into herself and hiding from his gaze the slim body he had enjoyed so thoroughly.

'I married you in good faith,' he said. 'It's unfortunate that I've taken for a wife a woman who now reminds me of my empty boyhood. I wanted us to have a child so in some measure that emptiness could be forgotten in the joy of making a child happy, but now when I look at you I can see the ghost of my mother and not for you, not for anyone will I cast aside my hatred. I can't help the way I feel, it's as simple as that!'

'Then for God's sake send me away—let me go home to England,' Linda begged of him. 'It's easy enough for you to divorce me. Do that and let the whole wretched experience be forgotten!'

'It isn't that easy . . .'

'Of course it is.' She looked up at him. 'If what you're concerned about happens, then I'll go for a termination.'

'A *what*?' His face went livid and stepping to where she sat he took her bruisingly by the shoulders. 'Do you really think I would permit such an abomination?'

'Why not?' She flung the fair hair back from her brow and braved his furious eyes. 'How can you want a child from me? How could you ever love it when you're so filled with hate?'

He glared down at her and her heart twisted inside her when she remembered how they had kissed each other, until they breathed as one person, not knowing whose heart did the beating for the pair of them. The lips that were now thin with anger had been fierce with desire, bold and insistent wherever they touched her until she had lain helpless in his arms, submissive to his every demand.

'Virgins,' she said quietly, 'don't always conceive at the start of the marriage—unless you are now going to accuse me of not being a virgin. You might as well paint me as black as possible.'

'It isn't a question of painting you black, Linda.'

His eyes slid over her white body which he had possessed so utterly. 'I am in no doubt that I took your virginity and there is no assurance in your statement that virgins don't always conceive—you will recall that we made love more than once. We made love a number of times.'

'Lovemaking?' She gazed up at him without a spark of illusion left in her eyes. 'You have the gall to call it that? All you did was to take my body—you didn't touch my heart, and if you think I'm going to stay here while you tick the days off the calendar then you had better think again. I have some pride! If you don't want me, then I'm going to leave you——'

She broke off with a cry as his hands crushed the bare flesh of her shoulders. 'You are going to do as you are told!' His brows were meshed together in a black frown and he had a look of total domination. 'In marrying you I made myself responsible for you—you and the child you might bear me. What is written has still been written even if a hand erases it, and until it suits me to say otherwise you will remain in my house, and if the seed has been sown you will bear my child.'

'A child you'll despise as much as you despise me.' Her voice faltered as she felt him against her, his warmth and power arousing the sensitive nerves inside her. Was he feeling the same sensations? Was he wishing they were on the bed together, kissing, touching, coming together in merciless rapture.

But she saw from the firm set to his features that he was in total control of himself. His resolution was equal to his passion and, unlike her, he wasn't new to passion. He was an experienced man and now she had become untouchable to him, he would probably assuage his needs elsewhere.

She pulled away and he allowed her to do so. As she

ran tremulous fingers through her hair her upraised arm tautened the line of her breasts and she felt his gaze upon their pliancy. Her midriff muscles contracted and she had a sudden wanton urge to recline on her back and perhaps break his resolve not to touch her. Oh God, she wanted him despite the gulf of coldness which had opened between them. She wanted the feel of his strong hands, stroking up her sides until his fingers found her breasts. She wanted his tawny body burningly close to her own, desirous and enslaving.

She could have sobbed with longing but she could see that Karim remained obdurate.

'So I've got to stay here even though you don't want me!'

'You aren't unwanted,' was his unexpected reply.

She looked up at him, her heart leaping, but his face was still hardset and she saw no glimmer of kindness in his eyes. Her own eyes questioned him, the pupils wide against the topaz irises, making them more beguiling than she knew.

'Forbidden,' he said, and then he walked away into the adjoining room and left her alone in the luxury of the bedroom where rapture had been replaced by rejection.

Suddenly Linda was recklessly angry again and running across to the other door she pulled it open and went inside. 'Forbidden? What do you mean by that, Karim? What is it supposed to mean—it sounds like something from the turn of the century and you—you're supposed to be a man of the world. It is just a pose and you're really like your forebears who put women into veils and harems and thought them good for only one thing—sex?'

'Sex is only a form of escapism,' he rejoined.

'Karim, I want an answer to my question not a thesis on something you seemed to thoroughly enjoy.'

'It was entirely enjoyable, Linda, I don't deny that.'

'But you're going to deny me, aren't you? All because of something I can't help. Look at me, does it make me any different to the person you saved on the road that day? That was the day, wasn't it, when you decided that you wanted me?'

'We were both misled in our expectations,' he said, almost savagely.

'You talk as if I deliberately misled you.' Linda looked at him and she couldn't believe he was the same man who had held her in his arms and made her feel so wanted.

'Perhaps you did mislead me.'

'How dare you say such a thing? You'll say next that I married you because you're a wealthy man.'

'Many girls have such an aim in life.'

'Karim, are you trying to make me hate you?'

'It might be better so.'

'I see.' Her face looked bleak as her anger drained away and was replaced by a kind of hopelessness, as if she were confronted by a towering cliff which would break her heart if she tried to reach its stony summit.

'If I hate you, Karim, then I suppose it might ease your conscience and make what you're doing to me seem right.'

'You are never going to understand, Linda.' The savagery was suddenly in his eyes. 'Maybe you would if you were Arabian.'

'You should have thought of that in the beginning, Karim. Didn't I say that you should marry a girl of your own nationality? You made the choice, my lord and master!'

And with this parting shot Linda went back into the

bedroom and slammed the door behind her. She seethed inside with a mixture of painful emotions while outwardly she trembled as if she would never feel warm again. Exhausted by the scene she sank down on the stool in front of the dressing-table and gazed at her white and miserable face in the mirror.

How long did misery last in adults? When she was ten years old it had lasted a long time and there wasn't a night when she hadn't cried herself to sleep. Again that desolate sense of abandonment swept over her and she leaned her head on her hands.

How, she wondered, was she going to face the days that lay ahead of her knowing that Karim would be watching for some sign that she had discovered herself to be pregnant or otherwise. How was she going to face the nights after discovering what a joy it was to share a bed with him?

With a sigh she arose and went into the bathroom of his suite. She turned on the shower and stepped beneath the down-beating water, wanting every kiss and every caress washed from her skin.

Teeth set she took hold of the bar of sandalwood soap and rubbed it all over her, then she scrubbed at her skin with the loofah until it was pink and tingling ... but what she couldn't do was to scrub away the memory of being so completely possessed that from now on every impulse of her body would have something of Karim in it.

She passed her hand over her wet stomach and stared into the mirrored wall at herself. She tried to see herself as Karim had seen her, slender and white-skinned, and sexually untouched until he had possessed her.

She shivered visibly at the memory of those hours in

his arms ... heaven which had turned into a kind of hell, and the very look of him had warned her that it could happen. She had known from the first moment she had set eyes on him that the ways of the desert were strong in his bones.

What was the decree of the Arab? An eye for an eye, a tooth for a tooth. Linda gazed into her own eyes and knew what was happening between her and Karim ... he had found someone to punish for what had happened to his parents; he had waited years to mete out that punishment.

As she wrapped a towel around herself, concealing the contours he had enjoyed, she prayed that her body wouldn't betray her by being pregnant with Karim's child.

If she became pregnant he would keep her here in his desert house and she didn't want to be the prisoner of his hatred.

When she returned to his bedroom she stood there indecisive. What should she do? Would it be considered etiquette in this household for her to return to her own bedroom? She decided that it might now the master of the house had enjoyed his privileges, and quickly she put on her dress, bundled up the veiling and the tunic and slipped out of the room.

In the shadowy depths of the colonnade she saw the white-clad figure of one of the household guards, but he had his back turned to her and the smoke of a cigarette was drifting over his shoulder. Linda passed him by like a shadow in the night and thankfully when she reached her own room it was empty and neither of her maids was there to wonder why she crept in so wanly.

She discarded the golden dress and replaced it with a night slip of cool transparent voile. She brushed her hair, drank some mineral water and slipped into her cool, tidy bed.

'Dear God,' she prayed, 'don't let me have a baby!'

CHAPTER SEVEN

LINDA awoke from a night of restless sleep and troubled dreams but when Perveneh came into the room with her breakfast tray she made an attempt to appear cheerful.

As the young maid approached her bedside with the tray there was a searching look in her brown eyes, a slight puzzlement that the Lady Linda was back in her own room and not beside the Sheikh on this the morning of her wedding night.

'*Café, lellah?*' The girl held the chased silver pot in readiness.

'Please.' Linda banked her pillows and sat against them, the hot morning sunlight playing over her ruffled hair and her pale shoulders from which the voile nightdress had slipped. She knew that she still looked outwardly the same but so much of her had changed inwardly. So many emotions chased each other through her system and her mind . . . for all time she had been changed into the sun lord's woman, but she was the woman he no longer felt free to touch.

While Linda drank her coffee Perveneh picked up the discarded dress in which the *lellah* had been married to his Eminence. Though the dress was crumpled and the veil still lay bundled with the gauze tunic Linda had carefully arranged the blue *babouches* on the dressing stool. The little amulet which Sofie had loaned her lay on the table at the bedside, her own chain of diamonds had been left behind in the Sheikh's bedroom, along with the lustrous gold bracelet which had always felt so heavy on her wrist.

Perveneh was trying to stroke the creases out of the gold dress when Sofie arrived. She came hurrying in with a smile on her lips but something in the atmosphere of the room cancelled her smile. She took the dress from Perveneh and glanced enquiringly at Linda. She wouldn't ask questions for that would be the height of discourtesy and Linda merely nibbled a warm and crusty roll to which she had added a little apricot jam and allowed the two Arabian girls to form the conclusion that British brides behaved in a different way from themselves.

After all, didn't the rest of the world know that the British were reserved and kept their deepest feelings to themselves? It wasn't altogether a fallacy and Linda had always been a person who locked away her hurts and disappointments and allowed a natural look of reserve to keep personal questions at bay.

'I'm sorry the dress got crumpled but I'm sure the creases will iron out.' She spoke lightly and knew that Sofie at least would guess that when the Sheikh had undressed her, he hadn't paused to hang her garments in the wardrobe. 'Thank you both for lending me the amulet and the slippers.'

'I will attend to the dress, my lady, and then with the other wedding garments it will be stored away. Such things are precious,' Sofie added with a touch of solemnity.

'Of course they are.' But Linda was trying to dismiss from her mind the image of herself as Karim's veiled bride. So far as she was concerned their marriage was annulled and she was going to have to find a way to get back to England.

How she was going to manage her escape Linda

didn't yet know but in the meantime she would make the best of an unhappy situation and try and enjoy the unusual city of Fez Eldjid. Her first glimpse of it the other day had aroused in her a desire to wander in the bazaar and visit the old palaces.

She would ask Karim to take her on a tour of the city ... even if they were no longer lovers they had to maintain a façade of intimacy for the sake of his eminent pride. He wouldn't want it to get around that they had already ceased to share a bed. For most men their *machismo* was an important aspect of their lives and Karim's very title of Sheikh meant leader and she had no wish to see him lowered in the esteem of his Arab friends.

For both their sakes she wanted to keep up the pretence of a marriage even if it was all an illusion ... the type of marriage she had sometimes glimpsed back home at the country club where in front of friends a couple would pretend to be brilliantly content with each other when all the time they were living inside a fragile shell that was cracking into pieces around them.

Linda's lips formed into a wry little smile. It was from that kind of atmosphere that she had fled and now she found herself living in the same kind of shell with Karim.

Where, she wondered, was happiness to be found? She had hoped to find it in Spain but on that winding road of fate El Khalid had been driving towards her and everything she had said to him last night was true, he had swept her off her feet and into this marriage without pausing to ask questions, and she wasn't going to be made to feel guilty.

She didn't feel in the least guilty about her mother but in a way she understood that all his life Karim had carried hatred in his heart for those who had robbed him of his parents. She, at least, had known what it was like to be cradled in her mother's warm arms and always when she went to bed Miriam would sing softly to her in the room with the sloping ceiling over which the night-light danced in shadows.

Linda was soaking in the bath when without any warning Karim strode in upon her. Perveneh gave him a curtsey and hastily left Linda alone with her husband.

'Good morning,' he said brusquely. 'We have to talk!'

'I know.' She sat there in the water not quite knowing what to do and he solved the matter by holding open a towel so she could climb out, just as on the evening at the castle when he had done the same thing. Only then he had been a total stranger to her, now as he enclosed her in the bath-towel he knew every aspect of her body whose slim pliancy could be pitched to a high degree of ecstasy.

As he pressed the towel against her wetness they were locked into a silence that was alive with their mutual awareness of each other; nothing could truly erase what had been written, and nothing could stop either of them from remembering the sensuous pleasures they had shared. Their sensory perception of each other had been acute and they were both aware of it.

He led her into the bedroom from which both her maids had vanished and he handed her the almond-green robe from the foot of her bed. She tied the sash and was aware that her nudity was revealed through the transparent fabric which was meant to be worn over a nightdress. She felt his eyes on her breasts, and then as if he couldn't help himself his gaze slid lower, and quite deliberately Linda didn't turn away from him.

Tiny muscles were contracting inside her and she wanted him to look at her, she wanted him to remember what it felt like when he took her in his arms and their bodies sought the intimacy that carried them out of their minds into a realm where pleasure blotted out the painful memories.

His gaze lifted to her ruffled hair that was very bright in the sunlight and she saw the nerves tugging at his lips. With all her heart and soul she willed him to cast aside the prejudice that was holding them apart, and then she saw his shoulders tauten against the indigo linen of his tunic as if he reinforced his resolve not to lay a finger upon her. At the same time his brown hands clenched into fists at the sides of his white Arab trousers swathed closely against the iron-hard muscles of his legs.

Linda shivered when she thought of his hands and the iron in those long legs that straddled the oriental carpet of her bedroom. They stood facing each other quite close to the bed and Linda was in awe of his control over himself . . . that same Eastern control that made him so marvellous a lover.

'Y-you said we must talk, Karim.'

'Yes.' He spread his hands in a fatalistic gesture. 'That is all we have left between us—talk.'

Linda stood there silently and disbelieved him; whatever his Arab conscience drove him to believe she knew that the physical side of him was clamouring to take hold of her. Those clenched hands of his were longing to glide over her skin and her skin was yearning for their touch.

A sigh escaped her and her breasts heaved in rhythm with it . . . instantly his eyes had focused on their uptilting shape through the sheer and clinging robe, and feigning a look of innocence Linda met his eyes and widened her own as if uncertain of why he looked at her in the way he did.

'You had better get dressed,' he said curtly.

'I am dressed, Karim.' She fingered the robe and gave him a look of bewilderment. 'This is one of the robes you were generous enough to buy me in Barcelona—you chose my things.'

'Yes, and it would seem that I chose them all too well.' He began to pace back and forth across the carpet, restless and driven as one of those sandcats who prowled in the desert. 'I would like you to put on something less provocative.'

'How can I provoke you, Karim, when there is nothing left between us?'

'Damn you!' He swung round and scowled at her, from head to heel an Arab who had left the Latin side of him behind in Spain; his nostrils flared as he came and stood over her and he half-raised a hand as if to strike her for contradicting him.

'Go on,' she said, her face tilted towards him, 'hit me, Karim, if it will help you to stop thinking of me as a woman.'

'In that garment how the devil can I stop thinking of you as a woman?' And then what she had incited happened, he reached for her and dragged her hurtfully close to him, his mouth descended and his lips took hers roughly. He kissed her in the same driven way he had paced the floor, bruising her intentionally with his angry mouth, uncaring that his grip left bruises on her body. Without removing his mouth from hers he backed her to the bed and crouched over her with all the fierceness and fury of a desert cat. The almond-green robe was pushed out of his way and savagely he took her, making no attempt to bring her to pleasure, assuaging his bitter anger because she had got under his skin with the sweet and lissom curve of her hips, the creamy pliability of her breasts, the sensuous innocence of her nature.

His anger wouldn't give way and the salt of his sweat ran across Linda's lips and his black hair clung to his brow ... *darling* was a silent cry inside her throat ... *my dear* had stolen into her heart beneath the hurtful grip of his fingers.

He fell away and lay with his back to her and though she wanted to put out her hand and soothe him she didn't dare invite his rejection of her touch. She straightened her robe and slid from the bed. Her legs were trembling as she went inside the big wardrobe and put on a cinnamon crêpe-de-chine shirt and a cream-coloured skirt. When she emerged he was standing by the meshwork windows smoking a cheroot and looking moody as the devil. Linda approached the dressing-table and combed her disordered hair into the troubador style that made her feel like Linda Layne instead of the Lady Linda whom this man had just treated as if she were a slut.

She stared at herself in the mirror as she applied a touch of make-up; she didn't really need any lip colouring for his angry kisses had left her lips aglow. And there deep inside her eyes was a matching radiance.

Whatever he did ... in whatever way he treated her there was some magic ingredient in the treatment that made the blood race joyously through her veins. From the edge of the mirror she could see him, big and dark and smouldering. Her heart missed a beat and her lips quivered with a tiny smile, and then the smile went away as she remembered the word he had used last night.

Forbidden!

'That was a nice scene, eh?' he muttered.

'It did the trick and I've changed my clothes, Karim.'

He cast a look at her, neat as a pin as she returned his look. 'By the Prophet you could deceive a saint!'

'And you're no saint, El Khalid.'

He drew deeply on the cheroot and the smoke made his eyes enigmatic. 'I've got to keep you here but it would seem that I'm unable to keep my hands off you.'

She slid her hands behind her and her fingernails dug into her palms. 'Best send me away then.'

'We both know I can't do that.'

'Why ever not? I only make you angry by being here.'

'You know why it's impossible.'

She gave a shrug which belied what she was feeling inside . . . now with every atom of her body she wanted to be with him. She wanted to see him big and dark each day. She wanted to know that he was within reach. She wanted him to make love to her even if he did it in anger. Like women down the ages Linda had discovered that it wasn't a man's insensitivity that hurt, it was his indifference, and the Sheikh el Khalid was not indifferent to her even if he didn't love her.

'I know what is possible,' she murmured.

He raised an enquiring eyebrow as he carried his cheroot to his lips and he seemed unaware that his black hair was still untidy on his brow.

'These scenes that we indulge in are bound to make happen what you say you don't want to happen—not any more, though it was your reason for marrying me.'

His moody dark eyes slid up and down her figure. 'I feel certain it happened yesterday.'

'Are you clairvoyant, Karim?'

'I don't have to be.' He gazed directly into her eyes. 'You are musical, you know when you have played a piece of music to perfection.'

One of those sensitive shivers ran all through her system. 'There are times when you say the most poetic things, Karim.'

'The desert soul harbours a flame of protectiveness and the pity to understand a sadness. I am not entirely made of stone, Linda.'

'I know that.' Her smile hung on the edge of sadness. 'I was there when we played our music.'

She heard him catch his breath, then from his pocket he produced her golden bracelet and he came to her and silently she held out her wrist while he secured it. He then took hold of her other wrist and discovered that her wristlet had long ago locked itself and couldn't be removed.

'I know how much you mind,' she said quietly, 'but it's all I have of my mother and though when I was a child I naturally couldn't understand why she left me and my father, I realise now I'm older that she probably found in the other man something she was unable to resist. No one is a saint and I—I can't help it if I still remember her big eyes and her lovely voice and can't bring myself to stop loving her. There's always a bond and you feel it, Karim, even though you never knew your mother.'

His strong fingers closed about her wrist and for seconds she thought he was going to wrench the little gold heart from her wristlet. 'You feel the impossibility of tearing out love from your heart for a mother who abandoned you of her own free will. I feel the impossibility of tearing out of my heart the hatred for those who inflict misery on the innocent.'

'Am I not innocent?' Linda asked him.

He stared down at her and graphic between them was the scene they had shared last night when he had learned about her mother. He let go of her wrist and once again he tramped back and forth across the room as if his restless thoughts would give him no rest.

'Tell me something, Linda, you are proud to be British, eh?'

'Of course,' she said, without any hesitation.

'I am proud to be of my father's people and you are right to consider me more of an Arab than a Spaniard. In any case the centuries of Moorish rule in Spain ensured strong blood links with the Arabs of Morocco and what we are is so deep inside us that it dictates all our thoughts and actions. At this precise moment, *berida*, I am an Arab who has for a wife a girl of the enemy—that is how my fellow Arabs would see it! If it was to become known then your life would be in danger—you saw those men at our marriage, they are the leaders of warlike tribes, men with whom I do business, men with whom I am in sympathy in many respects. Some of them despise the West but yesterday they saw you as a young and attractive woman whom I wish to have as my woman. They accepted the concession that you be at my side while the marriage service was performed, but you have to believe me, their anger would be deadly if they had an inkling of what I have learned. As I told you, hatred goes deep and though I don't expect you to understand the political reasons for that hatred, it is measured in terms of desert territory, home of the Arab since time began.'

She let his words sift through her mind and she remembered the proud, warlike faces of those robed men who had watched with enigmatic eyes while

Karim el Khalid had married her. Of all the nations of the West she was aware that the Arabian nation accepted the British more readily than they accepted others. Those men who were Karim's friends and compatriots accepted her as totally English, and she felt a stone cold chill go through her at the thought of being at the mercy of any one of them.

'What is going to happen to me?' she said in a lost sort of way.

Karim looked her up and down and she knew what he was seeing, a girl with a look which excited him physically . . . a girl who at this precise moment might be carrying his child. She saw a man who wasn't going to let go of her despite the dangers, not because he loved her but because of what had been potent between them from the very beginning.

When they touched nothing mattered except that they touch for hours on end. When they kissed they forgot everything but the kissing.

Last night he had used the word forbidden but this morning his desire for her had cancelled out the word and as he came towards her Linda felt her knees going weak. He reached her just in time to stop her from clutching at the bedpost for support . . . he pulled her to him and told her he would make arrangements for them to fly back to Spain.

'But I wanted to see something of Fez,' she protested.

'You aren't afraid?'

'I'm afraid but I'm not a coward.'

He held her away from him and searched her eyes. 'I'm tempted to test your courage.'

'I married you, didn't I?'

A smile flicked the edge of his lips. 'This evening when the day cools I shall commence your riding lessons, m'lady. Yes, I think we should stay here for a while, for if you are carrying my son then I want that son to be of the desert. There is no place on earth quite like it for it is man's glimpse of infinity.'

He drew her against his chest and her cheek brushed against the dark hair in the opening of his tunic. 'Where you are concerned, Linda, my resolves are not as strong as they should be, but then it's in the nature of man to desire the forbidden. I am not going to apologise for what occurred a while ago.'

'I'm not asking for your apology.'

'I was less than gentle with you.'

'I have never made the mistake of thinking of you as a gentle person.'

'What do you think of me, I wonder?' He gripped her head between his hands and tilted her face so it was exposed to his searching gaze. 'Do you care for me?'

'Do you want me to care?' she fenced.

'I don't know.' His eyes dwelt on her lips, sweetly wide and generous. 'I have never asked a woman to care for me with her heart.'

'You prefer a woman to care for you with her body?'

'Infinitely.'

'Then I shall do as my lord and master wants.' She shaped her lips into a smile but deep down inside she felt a touch of anguish. It had been inevitable that she would love his mastery over her ... in Linda as in Karim the sands of history ran deep and joined hands across that border where Judaic ideals clashed with those of the Moslem.

'Right now your master and lord wants his lunch. Come!' He gripped her by the hand and led her away to the roof of the tower where, in a while, their lunch was served to them on a table set up beside the thick, crennelated parapet that looked out over the tawny sands.

Now in daylight Linda saw that Karim's house stood on the very edge of the desert and from where she stood it seemed limitless. The vast desert baked golden by the sun, brooding and mysterious even in the light of day. Leagues of emptiness and a fierce purity in the air that she breathed. The sky overhead was a clear, translucent blue and to complete the picture she saw a string of camels coming in over the dunes.

'It's quite wonderful,' she exclaimed. 'Oh, Karim, I do want to stay—you won't change your mind?'

'I never change my mind, woman, once I have made it up.'

'You do, you know.' Linda swung round from the parapet and stood framed against the white stonework. 'You were so adamant last night when you said I was—forbidden.'

He inclined his head. 'A woman represents the one area of uncertainty where a man is concerned. We are both aware that the word crumbled to dust when I touched you.'

She felt that delicate shiver running over the sensitive strings of her inner being as she joined him at the table, where he was hungrily munching bread while he waited for their lunch to be brought to them. It proved to be delicious, starting with butter bean soup and going on to a dish of sliced potatoes alternating with layers of minced meat and onions topped by buttered potato, baked golden-brown. Once again Linda ate with a hunger she had never known before. In fact, now she thought about it, she seemed to have an increased appetite for everything . . . the things she looked at, the objects she touched, the sounds in the very air.

Across her cleared plate her eyes dwelt on Karim and she felt that same stirring of hunger for his shoulders that stretched open the indigo tunic to reveal his chest. He lifted his wine glass and her gaze was riveted to his hand and his lips, and she jumped visibly out of her thoughts when he spoke.

'Are you looking forward to your riding lesson?'

'Oh yes.' Her fingers fondled the stem of her own wine glass. 'I want to be able to ride with you in the desert, especially at night when it's cool and the stars come out.'

'They come out in their thousands, trailing their wildfire across the sky, but in the beginning we shall only take short rides because learning to ride can be tough on the thighs. Your maid will have to give you a massage. Arabian girls are adept with their hands.'

Linda ate fresh lime soufflé and considered his remark. Had there been many Arabian girls in his life; graceful, pretty girls like Sofie and Perveneh with an age-old instinctiveness when it came to pleasing a man physically. She must by comparison seem very untutored to him and she found there were questions in her mind clamouring for an answer ... questions which she had to suppress for the sake of her pride. She didn't want Karim to know that he had come to mean so much to her; that the very look of him could make her exultant because she belonged to him and he still wanted her despite his allegiance to his father's people.

She didn't care what it did to his conscience so long as they could be together as they were right now, with the unspoken promise of intimacy in the glances he gave her as they sat enjoying their Arabian coffee.

The sun glistened on her hair and its brightness seemed to fascinate him. 'You are so fair,' he said. 'One would think of you as entirely Anglo-Saxon.'

'My grandfather was a big blond man—I told you it was in Holland where he was interned. My mother had the most gorgeous blonde hair when she was young and she used to wear it in shining scrolls that rested on her shoulders. She loved the night life of being a dance band singer and I suppose that was why she never settled down to a domestic routine.'

'Your relatives in England will soon receive the news that you are now a Sheikha.'

'Yes.' She looked right into his eyes and as always when there was distance between their faces he seemed aloof. 'Are you tremendously sorry about our marriage? What will you do if I find out I'm not going to have a child—please tell me, Karim! Be frank with me!'

'I shall probably have the knot untied.' He held her gaze relentlessly. 'But I shall see to it that you don't need to work as a *compañera*, your settlement, I promise you, will be more than generous and you will be enabled to continue with your musical studies. I would want you to do that.'

'Would you?' With all her might Linda strove not to show him how much his words had hurt her, penetrating like a knife into those sensitive and sensuous areas where he had awoken her to the pleasures of being a woman. No doubt she could live without him but it seemed a bleak prospect, and strangely enough she didn't reverse the prayer which had been on her lips last night.

She didn't want his child just for the sake of holding on to him; if already he was thinking in terms of untying the knot which so tenuously bound them, then better for both of them that it be untied. In the meantime he would enjoy her, and she recklessly told herself that it would be a memory worth taking back to

Essex . . . the memory of her days and nights with her Arabian lover.

Nothing so ardent or so adventurous would happen to her ever again and she resolved to enjoy every moment of being the sun lord's woman.

Gaily she broke into a smile and reached into the bowl of fruit for a tangerine, as her fingers idly moved aside the other items of fruit something scuttled out of the bowl on to her arm and quick as black lightning it ran to her shoulder and never in her life had Linda let out such a scream. She leapt to her feet and ran wildly to the wall of the tower.

'Get it off! Get it off!' she screamed, and Karim had to hold her still while he plucked the huge spider off her blouse. She crouched against the parapet while he dropped the thing into an empty wine glass and carried it away, ringed, black-furred, hideously bow-legged and with awful little eyes.

Linda couldn't stop brushing at herself and her skin was still crawling when Karim returned and took her straightaway into his arms, where she twitched with nervous reaction. 'It's all right, child,' he stroked her hair, 'there wasn't time for it to bite you.'

She shuddered at the very thought. 'Oh, Karim, w-where did it come from?'

'It was probably enticed into the bowl by the aroma of the fruit, now tell me, are you feeling better?' He raised her face to his and scanned its whiteness. 'Little one, you gave such a scream!'

'Ugh!' She buried her face in his warm chest. 'I—I don't know what I'd have done if I had been on my own—how could you pick it up—I'd die if I had to do that!'

'No you wouldn't.' He dropped a kiss on her hair. 'In all hot climates the creatures exist and the bite of that species isn't fatal, though it causes a fever. Scorpions are much deadlier and have a nasty habit of crawling into footwear so always be sure to shake out your shoes or boots before putting them on. The bite of the scorpion can be fatal.'

'Oh dear,' she pressed close to his strength and his sureness, 'the desert only looks peaceful but it harbours quite a few terrors, doesn't it?'

'You will accustom yourself to the creepy crawlies.' He stroked her where the spider had been as if to exorcise with his touch the sensation of the furred legs on her skin. This time when she shivered it was with a different kind of feeling, and with a soft, throaty laugh Karim lifted her into his arms and carried her down the winding steps of the tower. She clung to his shoulders, her head buried against him, knowing exactly what his intention was.

In the master suite the fans purred and sent cool air wafting round the rooms. He lazily smoked a cigar while Linda wandered among his belongings, feeling his eyes upon her as she examined his books, his hunting trophies, and the pictures on the walls. She knew more about music than painting but the theme of his collection didn't surprise her; they were all paintings of the desert, burningly alive with colour and strange rock formations . . . a land, she thought, which the hand of modern man couldn't bend to his will.

She swung to face Karim, lounging at his ease on a wide divan covered by a huge striped pelt. She carefully approached and fingered the pelt, which felt like rough velvet. 'Tigerskin?' she asked.

Karim inclined his head. 'A magnificent creature but a killer who had to be killed. He fell to my gun in the hills of India, a cunning devil who used to creep into one of the hill villages just as the women started to cook supper on their open fires and he'd snatch one of their infants while they were occupied. It is said that tigers are afraid of fire but this one was undeterred. Come, sit beside me.'

Linda did so, pulling up her legs and resting against a big soft cushion. His eyes rested on the ankle that still wore the slender chain of hearts and he extended a hand and closed it around her other ankle.

'You like a touch of barbarity, don't you?' he murmured. 'I have noticed that you don't say the usual things that leap so readily to the tongues of city women, whose only contact with wild animals is the occasional venison steak or mink wrap. You understand that I speak of the European woman who is likely to be found at the Hilton Hotel or the Inter-Continental. My contact with your kind of girl didn't happen until that day on the road to the *castillo*.'

'I must seem so unsophisticated by comparison,' she murmured.

'Totally,' he agreed, and his fingers softly stroked her leg. 'You are unpretentious and you react with a sincerity which I find very novel and very refreshing. When you kiss a man you mean it, and when you strike a man you mean it.'

He watched her through the smoke of his cigar and the lids of his eyes were lazily contemplative. 'Such passion in such a slim white girl—usually, you know, I find European women a little bloodless.'

'Have there been many?' She just couldn't hold back the words.

'A reasonable number,' he mocked. 'You surely wouldn't take me for a man who has lived like a monk, would you?'

'Hardly.' Her eyes dwelt on his lips and she felt

twinges of jealousy at the thought of him kissing and
possessing other women, and those twinges sharpened
as she envisioned the yielding, helpless pleasure of
other women in his arms, their hands stroking his
brown shoulders, wandering down over his muscular
body.

Suddenly, as if reading her thoughts, he leaned
forward and drew her to him. She gazed up at him and
lifted a hand to stroke the sideburns that slashed
darkly against his lean cheekbones. She trailed a finger
across the detailed bones of his face and traced with a
fingertip the proud structure of his nose. Slowly and
sensuously she stroked the column of his neck. Close
like this Linda could feel the acceleration of his
breath, and she started to kiss him, trailing her lips
where her fingers had wandered, budding them and
pressing them into his skin, the tip of her tongue
sliding along the hard bone of him.

Because she had grown up in a household where
affection wasn't often demonstrated Linda hadn't
realised the glory of showing affection. The look of
Larry Nevins had never moved her and his kisses had
felt dry as a paper napkin.

But, oh, how she loved the warm brown of Karim's
skin, and when she brushed her lips across his eyes she
could feel the thickness of his lashes tickling against
her mouth. She longed to explore all of him and he
silently carried her into the bedroom and within
seconds their clothing seemed to peel off and he drew
her down upon him with a lazy welcoming smile.

She stroked the dark hair that branched across his
chest and descended to his hard stomach. 'You feel
like a tigerskin,' she shyly told him.

He ran his hands up the creamy sides of her body
and urged her towards him so he could tease with his

lips the tips of her breasts. He sent wild thrills coursing through her and his eyes enticed her to a playfulness that all at once became a natural and joyous expression of her needs.

Her creamy body blended into his and together they created the markings of the tiger, rippling in the sunlight and the shadow of their private domain.

There was nothing beyond being with him . . . the warm wildness, the hammering heart against her, the dear proud head clutched to her, they made up for everything. The lonely ten-year-old child had stolen away and in her place a woman enjoyed to the full the passion she had let loose in the man.

'He'll never send me away,' she told herself. 'No one will ever love him as much as I do.'

In a suspended moment of passion he stroked the hair from her brow and looked down into her wide pupils ringed with gold. 'My wild, wild little falcon,' he breathed.

'Oh yes,' she said, and they flew off the rim of their own high cliff into the ancient fire of the sunset that filled the room.

CHAPTER EIGHT

MOONLIGHT lay across the sands, the moon having risen brilliantly from behind the rock faces which the winds had sculptured into awesome profiles, like ancient gods of the desert.

All around them as they rode side by side the moon shadows lay like lace on the sands and the air which Linda breathed was intoxicatingly fresh after the heat of the day. She had discovered in herself a love of riding and she had proved a good pupil from the moment Karim had assisted her into the saddle of Farida, a beautiful auburn mare with a black mane and tail. It wasn't that Farida was docile, for like Karim's black stallion Malik she was pure Arabian, but Linda had approached her and climbed into her saddle without a trace of fear and something in her English voice seemed to appeal to the mare who pranced at first and swished her tail.

Now five weeks later Linda was at home in the saddle and each day she looked forward to these gallops across the sands after the sun had left the sky and the brazen desert turned to nightshade purple.

'I never get tired of the beauty of it all.'

Karim turned his head to give her his cryptic smile . . . a smile which held the power to set her wondering, for even after being with him for several weeks Linda still found him a man who was like the desert itself, whose silences were as fascinating as its storms, with a beckoning quality which could also be forbidding.

'It pleases me, *berida*, that you find the desert

beautiful. Look up at the stars, even the moon can't eclipse them.'

They lay across the vault of heaven in great clusters of silver fire that lit Linda's face to a pallor that was deceiving; in daylight her skin had acquired a tan and the sun had brightened her hair almost to platinum. She looked and felt a different person from the one who had arrived at the *Ras Blanca* feeling so nervous of marriage with El Khalid.

By now she was well acquainted with the big fine body in the loose tunic and swathed Arab trousers, his cloak making patterns in the air as the wind got inside it. She could feel her own cloak tugging at her shoulders, for the desert was a strange place. All of a sudden it could grow as cold as an English dawn and she was always glad to wrap the cloak tightly around her as she and Karim rode homewards.

She felt her heart beating with a deep sense of belonging, and yet it was only transient. Karim hadn't asked but she believed he had guessed that she wasn't carrying his child. Their lovemaking was a flame touching silk; they had even made love in the desert under the stars, but she knew for certain that she wasn't pregnant. She had prayed not to be so and in a way that prayer still held good. She wanted Karim to want her for herself alone and she tried her best to be a fulfilling companion for him, both day and night.

They rode towards the ridge where they usually rested the horses while Karim smoked a cigar. She liked the rich tang of the smoke mingling with the night air, and she loved the way he would gaze across the vast spaces as if he could never feast enough on the desert. He knew it in peace and battle, and Linda had lived with him long enough to know when he was brooding on the ghost that sometimes walked between them.

As he leaned against a wind-sculpted pillar and carried a flame to his cigar she could see that he had something on his mind. He smoked about an inch of his cigar before he spoke.

'Tomorrow,' he said, 'I have to go to Rabat to attend a meeting of the Sheikhs and you will be alone for about a week. Tell me, do you want to stay in Fez or would you like to return to Spain? I could join you there when these talks are over and done with.'

'Do you want me to go to Spain, Karim?' She flicked her riding stick against her boot and didn't look at him directly.

'I would prefer that,' he said. 'You know why I don't much like the idea of you being alone at the *Ras Blanca*.'

'I'm not nervous, Karim.' She met his eyes through the cigar smoke that wafted between them. 'You know I like it here in Fez and a week soon passes.'

'Then so be it.' He made a fatalistic movement with his left hand. 'I am aware that the desert has got into your blood and you never complain about the heat or the sand flies and the occasional hot wind that carries grains of sand into the house. You are a rather rare creature for a woman.'

His eyes moved up and down her slim figure in the boyish riding clothes and she saw that secret little smile creep into his dark eyes lit by the moon. 'You have your piano, so you won't miss your husband, eh?'

'No, master, I shall play Chopin to my heart's content.' Her lips quivered into a smile. 'It was the kindest thing on earth, Karim, buying me that beautiful Beckstein and having it shipped over from Barcelona.'

'I like to hear you play and a piano is an instrument which only needs a player and a listener. The cello needs the company of violins and other cellists.'

'I wish I could give you something,' she murmured, and she was half regretful that she couldn't say to him here and now that she was going to have his baby. It was why he had married her but it was no longer the reason why they stayed married. Despite his wealth and his position there was inside him some of the loneliness of the desert and she tried to erase it. Perhaps she did, for in his sleep he would reach across the big bed and enclose her with his arm. The movement would sometimes awaken her but Karim never awoke himself and she would in the silence of the night enjoy the luxury of pretending that nothing would ever separate them.

But it was only a luxury for there were other times when he paced the flagstones of the courtyard, withdrawn into thoughts she dare not intrude upon. She knew he was haunted by memories deep in his subconscious. The violence and the brutal slaying of his father, witnessed by his mother, had transmitted itself to him and he was unable to forget, unable to forgive, for all in all he was an Arab, and there were occasions when he would grip hold of the little heart on Linda's wrist and his features would look ominous.

Linda was deeply afraid of those nights when he left her to sleep alone in the kingly bed where it was possible to be totally intimate or lazily apart in the delicious silence with only the ceiling fans purring away like satisfied cats.

She was too aware of the shadow that lay over his thoughts, when for hours he would allow the chastisement of his ghosts to drive him away from her. She would kneel like a waiting slave on the window divan and watch him through the intricate meshes of wrought iron, for she had long since learned that he had turned the *haram* of the house into the master suite.

Most of the rooms in the *Ras Blanca* were beautiful, but the bedroom she shared with Karim was the most decorative of all. The lotus blossom symbol of eternal youth was used with great imagination in the carving of the bedposts that reared all the way to the high ceiling. She would fondle the carved lotus petals when she lay at ease at his side, smiling a little to herself, feeling not unlike his *robija*.

She was, after all, a slave of her senses when Karim touched her; the very feel of his lean brown hand on her skin was enough to scatter her thoughts like doves from the fretwork tower, for when he touched her they shared a world that was entirely their own. Nothing and nobody was allowed to intrude, and it amazed Linda the way his household was run, so unlike her aunt's house where the meals were served punctually at the same time each day.

Here in Karim's desert house they ate at midnight if it suited his whim and his staff never seemed to mind. They would serve a four-course meal, then whip away the plates with silent courtesy, and if it amazed them to hear the music of Chopin stealing through the colonnades of the house until the early hours of the morning they never showed their amazement.

She was the Lady Linda who pleased their Sheikh. She wore evening dresses which revealed her arms and shoulders and often deep areas of her slender back. She rode with him in the desert dressed like a boy in breeches and shirt and kneeboots. She made a strange music with her fingers which their lord and master seemed to find absorbing.

The days and nights at *Ras Blanca* were memories
strung on golden threads but Linda was always
prepared for the sudden shock of being told by Karim
that he had decided to send her away.

Now in the starlit desert she studied his face and
wondered if his trip to Rabat was the beginning of the
end for them. He had suggested that she return to
Spain and restlessly she walked away from him to
where a group of palm trees waved their fans in the
night breezes.

All at once she decided to put into words what was
unspoken between them. 'You know, don't you,
Karim, that I'm not going to have a baby?'

'Yes, I know.'

'Do you mind or are you relieved?'

'I haven't given it very much thought.'

'You threatened to untie the marriage knot if I
didn't fall for a baby.'

'I expect the day will come,' he rejoined, and his
voice sounded distant to her.

She shivered and drew her cloak around her, but
she had resolved never to mention the word love. She
never did, not even when he made her feel like
screaming it when she lay in his arms and there wasn't
an inch of her body that wasn't alive with joy, lapped
by tiny flames of pleasure, that grew into one
engulfing flame, that scorched her to him so they
clung and burned as if in the centre of some pure
white star shooting through the spaces of infinity.

It was a feeling akin to the exultation in music and
just as she had never grown weary of listening again
and again to her favourite composers so she never
grew weary of those first expectant moments when
Karim drew near and laid his hand upon her.

He did it now and she lifted wide and startled eyes

to his face. 'Don't think,' he murmured, 'just feel.'
And he drew her down upon the sands and opened her
cloak and his hands were so warm and aware against
her skin as he slowly unbuttoned her shirt. She stirred
and arched like a slender cat as he caressed her body,
and as always she reached out to him for the touch of
his skin was somehow wonderful to her. So living and
alive over the flesh and bone of him and because she
had sensitive, musician's hands Linda was aware that
she gave him extraordinary pleasure. He had likened
her to a mistress of the arts, smiling as he said it but
with a look in his dark eyes that imparted his delight.

The desert was a pool of black and silver shadows as
Linda gave herself to Karim and was taken fiercely by
him. Here in the desert he was totally Arabian and
they were on the eve of their first parting since the day
of their marriage.

They were an Arab with his woman on the sands
where time stood still, their sleek mounts making
music with their bridles as they stood tethered but
unconcerned in the garden of shadows. The stars
shimmered in Linda's eyes as she clung to Karim's
powerful shoulders and gave him her heart as well as
her body. What did it matter if he didn't know or care
that she had come to love him beyond reason? She
wasn't by far the first woman to love and not be loved,
and the little gold heart on her wrist was sheened by
the moonlight, tiny and mocking as it swung to the
rhythm of her stroking hands on the brazen body of
her lover.

'Oh—yes.' Her fingernails stabbed him, always
leaving their crescents as mementos of passion.
'Darling—darling——'

He rested his face in the velvety valley between her
breasts and his warm gusts of breath tickled her skin.

She stroked his dark head and they lay like the moonlight on the sands, with not a slither of space between their intermingling.

In a while he leaned upon an elbow and gazed down into her eyes where the pupils were held within their rims of gold. 'You have the most infinitely sweet body in the world,' he murmured. 'I go a little out of my head but I don't mean to bruise you.'

'We both leave our mark, don't we?' she slowly smiled.

He quirked a black eyebrow, then lowered his head to her moonlit breasts where his warm lips teased her until live wires seemed to thread her body. They both knew, though it remained unspoken, that her ability for passion was due to her divided parentage. Her cool blonde looks concealed a flame and deep within her genes she felt no stranger to the desert sands where she lay in Karim's arms and enjoyed his kisses on her body.

His hands stroked over the fine silken texture of her hips and he slowly raised her towards him and she felt the quickening of his body and the sudden stab of dazzling pleasure.

They cantered homeward with their cloaks drawn closely around themselves, holding in the warmth against the sudden coldness that filled the night. In the courtyard of the house he lifted her slowly from the saddle and let her body glide down against his own. They were seized by a mutual shudder between sensuality and some other indistinct feeling.

The stable hand took the horses and as Karim walked with Linda into the house his hand pressed against the Hand of Fatma that was incised into the wall beside the arched entrance. He didn't always do this and it faintly worried Linda that he should do it tonight. She wanted to throw her arms around him; she wanted to plead with him not to go to Rabat where talks of significance were going to be held, but she hadn't full rights over a man who merely kept her with him because she pleasured him . . . just as the women of the harems had pleasured other men of his stamp. Fierce, proud masters of the East in whose very marrow was bred a liking for danger and a belief that a woman was born to be a source of delight.

'So you will stay in Fez while I'm away from you?' He asked the question as they sat in the *sala* sharing a delicious dish of *cous-cous*, a mound of spicy semolina studded with tender chunks of chicken and vegetables.

She nodded and opened her lips to receive a piece of chicken from his fingers. 'Please let me, Karim. I shall feel closer to you.'

'Then as I said before, *berida*, so be it.'

'I don't often oppose your wishes, do I, m'lord?' She smiled into his eyes, her heart melting with love of his face.

'Unlike other women you have no side that is prickly as cactus, that I can say for you.'

'Thank you, m'lord.'

'You are welcome, m'lady.'

Later he smoked while she sat among cushions and ate nuts and fruit. The desert air made her continually hungry and though she was always nibbling something, especially the delectable almond cakes which were one of the cook's specialities, she never seemed to put on an ounce of superfluous flesh. It pleased her. While she kept her shape and seemed never to be enervated by the daytime heat she knew that she held Karim in physical thrall to her. It meant that she always looked slim and fresh and could respond to him whenever he felt a need for her.

Despite the hazard of being Miriam's daughter, Linda exulted in the fact of it. She had her mother's nature and could hardly bear to think what she would have been like as a person had Aunt Doris been her mother. She felt quite certain that by now she had become as much of an outcast to her family as Miriam had always been. Her name was probably never mentioned any more, and it sometimes gave her an odd feeling when she realised that she had no home except the one she shared with Karim.

In more ways than one she was at his mercy.

She leafed through a book of Koranic script on gazelle skin and nothing could alter the fact that no matter how often she was physically close to El Khalid he remained as much of an enigma as the beautiful red and gold lettering at which she gazed. She wanted to understand his language and she yearned to understand Karim himself, but they both eluded her.

With a little sigh she returned the book to its place among his other books, some of them in English and several featuring that most formidable of Englishmen, Winston Churchill. There was also a volume of verse by Robert Browning and she felt like asking her husband why he read love poems when he had dismissed from his own heart any feelings of love.

'What will you do while I'm away?' he asked her.

'I'm going to explore the city——'

'Not alone!' he rapped.

'No, I shall go with Sofie and don't worry, Karim, I shall be sure to wear the enveloping *abayah* and no one will know me from any other Arabian woman. I want to see the silk market and the snake dancing and I—I might have my fortune told by the teller of fates.'

'Ah, you are a child,' he half-smiled.

'You didn't think so while we were in the desert,' she reminded him.

'No, in that area you are Circe herself.'

'Winding my coils of enchantment around you?'

'Silken white and golden coils, *mia farah.*'

She knelt down again upon the velvety pile of the carpet and the lamps in distant corners of the *sala* emitted a spicy scent, not strong but constant. Tonight she wore an orchid-pink chiffon tunic bordered in glowing pearl embroidery and her hair was softly unarranged, and the divine echoes of desire still sang in her veins.

Karim beckoned her and she went and sat close to his legs, like a kitten, she thought, content with just one person in the entire world of people.

'Would you like a present?' he asked.

I would like you to love me, she thought to herself. She laid her cheek against his swathed knees. 'Not long ago you gave me my lovely piano.'

'This is different.' He handed down to her a hammered gold box and when Linda opened it, disclosed on a bed of plush was a Hand of Fatma in purest jade.

'Karim, how perfectly lovely!'

'It will safeguard you while I'm away, your own personal *feisha.*'

She lifted it out of the box and found that it was suspended on a chain fine as a golden hair, and she played with the jade charm in her fingers, watching how the light in the jade played a green shadow over her own hand.

'You are generous, Karim.' She reached for his hand and pressed a kiss into his palm. 'What do I give you in return?'

'More than you know,' he replied.

'My body?'

'A delicious body.'

She slid into the circle of his arm and he fastened the *feisha* about her neck, his fingers holding it a moment then gliding down to enfold her beneath the chiffon. His fingertips brushed her, softly back and forth, and all the time his eyes brooded on her face through the black veil of his lashes.

'I have seven nights of loneliness ahead of me,' he said.

For silent moments she listened to her own breathing as he continued to fondle her ... was it remotely possible that he would fill those nights with someone else? Some other soft and willing body that he would hold close to his warm vibrancy and bring to a pitch of almost tortured pleasure?

It was sheer agony for Linda to even think of him doing such a thing. It would be like a betrayal, a treachery, and yet she hadn't the right to wring promises from him.

'I—I shall be lonely as well.'

'Then we had better provide ourselves with a feast before the famine begins.' With supple strides he carried her along the colonnade where the goldfish made plopping sounds among the night-closed buds of the water-lotus. With a little surge of desperation Linda closed her lips upon the earlobe closest to her ... she would send Karim away with such a memory of this night that he would look at other women in Rabat and see them only as sticks.

He had left for Rabat before Linda awoke in the morning, when already the sun was high. She felt instantly a sense of loneliness. She had wanted to kiss him goodbye and the note pinned to his pillow added to her sense of regret.

She read what he had written. *The famine now begins and I shall fast until we hold each other in the fastness of the night.* She pressed the slip of paper to her lips, her toes curling into the silk sheet as intimate images of him slid through her mind, her very own private screen which she never grew tired of viewing. She read his note again and gave a little sigh that he hadn't signed it with his love.

It was as if Karim, separated so soon from his mother, had never learned how to open his heart to love. He enjoyed to the full the use of his magnificent body but love was a word that never passed his lips.

He paid her warm compliments relating to her hair, her skin, her slender shape; he told her in the most sensual terms that she pleased him, but he never unlocked his heart and invited her inside. He had never intimated that their relationship had more depth to it than the purely physical; he seemed satisfied with their marriage on that level and Linda tried her hardest not to remember why they had quarrelled on their wedding night.

She tucked his note into the little golden box which had held her *feisha,* still on its golden chain around her neck and there to stay, and decided that she would cheer herself up by going to the bazaar with Sofie and Perveneh.

When the two girls arrived, one with her breakfast and the other with a freshly laundered riding shirt, she gaily informed Sofie that they were all going into the city because she wanted to have her fortune told. 'I want one of those mysterious old men to read my fate in the grains of sand,' she announced.

Sofie gave her a slightly troubled look but didn't

argue with her, and later on the three of them left the house clad in their *abayahs*, the street garment which concealed women behind intriguing eyeslits of lace. They entered the big car with the covered windows and drove towards the city where Linda told the driver to drop them off and wait for their return.

Behind her veiling she was smiling to herself. There was a strange kind of excitement to being the wife of a Sheikh, and she could understand why so many Moslem women clung to the traditional veil. It made them seem mysterious and unattainable, unlike European women who in their bikinis managed to look like sides of meat on sale.

Walking between the two Arabian girls Linda entered the city of Fez beneath the great archway where once upon a time the heads of transgressors had been spiked so others could learn a lesson from the horrible sight. Beyond the ancient red walls the city teemed with noise and the narrow streets were alive with people wandering among the covered stalls.

The streets were made narrower by the houses that overhung them, their walls patched and scaled by the hot sun that was diluted among the stalls by the reed awnings. There were no windows on the lower floors of the houses and, as Linda knew, much of the life of a family went on colourfully on the flat rooftops.

The thronged streets led into the heart of the bazaar and veiled as she was Linda could study the milling people to her heart's content. Some of the faces were beautiful but others were barbaric, as if their owners came in from the mountains where the Berbers were still very warlike. Her own husband was a Berber on his father's side and often she had seen the same look of pride intermixed with an air of ruthlessness which warned those around to keep their distance.

Slippered merchants wrapped in their robes tried
to interest the three young women in their assortment
of goods, some of which looked enticing until Sofie
whispered to Linda that it was overpriced junk and
she would do better to save her money until they
reached the *souk* of silks and the shop where she
could have a scent blended to her very own skin
aromas.

'Oh, I must do that,' she said, and the excitement of
the bazaar had soothed away her earlier feeling of
despondency. 'And you will take me to see a teller of
fates?'

'If the *lellah* so wishes.'

'You seem—reluctant, Sofie.'

'They are clever men and they can see things.' Sofie
looked at Linda through the lace that covered her
eyes. 'The *lellah* must be certain that she wants the
future uncovered for her.'

'I—think I do.' Linda wasn't altogether certain that
she believed in fortune tellers but it would be
interesting and the sand diviner might even tell her that
her future was going to be an oasis of happiness.

For now she lost herself in the displays of vivid
garments and slippers meant entirely for indoor wear;
she handled leather bags that felt unbelievably soft,
and admired fretted silver lamps. The vendors would
study her with avarice in their eyes and several times it
was only the persistent grip of Sofie or Perveneh that
saved her from buying something she would have little
use for when she took it home.

In the house of Sheikh el Khalid, as the two
Arabian girls well knew, there were treasures that
outshone market wares, and with a laugh Linda
allowed them to lead her away; they didn't quite
understand that in some respects she was a tourist and

like other visitors was beguiled by the exotic things on display.

Quite a number of European visitors were wandering in the alleyways and it amused her to see the men glance at a trio of veiled women and wonder what the draperies concealed. She wondered what the reaction would be if she suddenly uncovered her fair head and revealed herself as a European.

'I'm enjoying this,' she confided to Sofie, 'wandering about in a veil. It makes me feel mysterious.'

Sofie smiled and obviously understood the implication. The wrapped package was more exciting than the uncovered one, and then all at once Linda paused to pick up a pair of baby slippers made of silk-soft leather in a pale primrose colour. 'Enchanting,' she exclaimed. 'Look how the tiny toes curl upwards— these I am going to buy!'

She proceeded to do so and was amusedly aware of Sofie and Perveneh glancing at each other as if wondering if their mistress was with child. 'You never know.' She tucked the slippers away in her woven basket. 'The teller of fates might inform me that I'm going to have half a dozen lusty children.'

She dropped coins into the begging bowl of an old man seated near the doorway of one of the beautifully tiled mosques where just inside the shaded entrance a group of students were chanting their lessons. She stood in total fascination and watched a sinister looking snake dancer twirl to the music of flute and finger-cymbals, the mottled snakes gliding around his body, hissing and showing their fangs. He had the marks of bites all over him, white against his blue-black skin, and though Linda suspected that the venom had been withdrawn from the snakes it was still a skin-crawling spectacle.

There were sellers of amulets, beads, bangles and curved knives wickedly jewelled. Large wickerwork panniers emitted the aromas of spices, herbs and a mixture of fruits. The figs looked delicious and again Linda dipped into her purse and bought some. Her two companions again shook their heads at each other as if to say that she was the mistress of a rich house with a kitchen full of food and yet, rather like a child, she had to buy figs in the market.

'I know they'll have to be washed and washed,' she said to Sofie, 'but they are so luscious looking.'

Oh, to be a painter, she thought as she looked around her at this walled city which time had trapped in the amber of the Arabian sun. Houses leaning one against the other for support, minarets that speared the turquoise sky, and ramparts that echoed with the street noises.

By now there were several inches of dust on her *abayha*, thrown upwards by the shuffling slippers of the people that passed back and forth, some laughing, others muffled to the eyebrows. There was the tap of hammers on brass and copperware, and within his bit of space a man sat painting designs on pots and plates of all sizes, and beside him there was a mint-seller, his baskets piled high with the aromatic herb which the Arabians loved to put in their tea. Linda had grown to enjoy the taste and found mint-tea very refreshing.

She felt attuned to the pulse and throb of the activity around her, as if in being part of Karim she had absorbed a liking for the throaty speech, the vivid gestures, the dark and dangerous eyes that seemed to see the shape of a woman through the concealing street robe.

How far removed Linda thought wonderingly from the sedate life with her aunt and uncle, with its ordered routine that extended from the houses into the tree-lined roads and the shopping precinct where the bargaining and bartering that went on in the bazaar was unheard of. In certain areas of London there were markets not unlike this one in Fez, but Linda's life until she met Karim had followed a regulated pattern of music study and then the train ride home in the evening to the house in which she had pined for colour and warmth.

In the *souk* of silks she was overwhelmed by the lovely, hand-loomed fabrics in every shade and variation of the rainbow. She insisted that Sofie and Perveneh choose lengths for themselves to be made up by Sofie into dresses. They were delighted and while they did their selecting Linda wandered around on her own, stroking the silk, the damask, the velvet and the lacework. She finally bought for herself a lacy stole in a shadowy deep-lilac that reminded her of the desert at night, the garden of Allah where she had lain in Karim's arms and adored his face by moonlight. Surrendering to his desire with every nerve and cell of her body.

She drew the lace through her fingers, knowing right now that she loved the man, loved his land, and his people. They had a strength and a mystery that appealed to a deep centre of herself that was her true inheritance from Miriam. In her very veins there beat an Eastern rhythm from long, long ago. It was why she and Karim were never strangers when they touched, it was because they shared an affinity which like the desert itself was timeless. From the first instant they had looked at each other that affinity had mastered both of them, and standing here, breathing the aroma of dye from the silk vats, Linda gloried in her discovery.

She loved Karim . . . he was the rib of Adam from which she had grown to become his woman. The sun lord's woman!

Smiling, she told Sofie that having bought silk for them she now wanted to buy a gift for the Sheikh. She had decided on a leather belt stamped with a Koranic prayer which he could wear around his tunic. 'A good prayer, Sofie. A prayer with meaning.'

So they went to the dealer in leatherware and he showed her belts in a range of shades and widths, some of them stamped with designs, others stamped with Koranic script. The belt she selected was teakcoloured and the script was in gold-leaf and the prayer stated simply; *Blessed be the man of loving heart.* It was costly and Linda had just enough money left in her purse to pay a teller of fates.

'I'll buy scent another time. Let's go and find a sand diviner who looks like Merlin the Wizard.'

They found him in the carpet square, seated on the ground near the mounds of marvellous oriental carpets, rich and lustrous from the far corners of the East, and Sofie explained that her mistress was from England and she wished the diviner to read her fate in the sands of Arabia.

CHAPTER NINE

THE old man of the East gazed up steadily at Linda, peering with his sharp little eyes into the lace slits that partly concealed her eyes, then he spoke to Sofie in a voice as rasping as sand grains when the wind blew them across the courtyard of the *Ras Blanca*.

Sofie turned to Linda and told her what the diviner had said, that he would much like to read in the sand the fate of a *roubia* who on the surface had much to be envied.

Linda felt startled. 'How does he know I'm a blonde?'

'Guesswork, I think, *lellah*,' Sofie replied in Spanish. 'Do you want him to go on?'

'Oh yes.' Linda was in no doubt. 'He looks as old as the hills and wise as an owl, and will be fun even if he tells me a lot of rot.'

Sofie told the old man to proceed and he took from his grubby robes a drawstring bag from which he poured a little mound of sand. He stirred it around with a forefinger on which the nail was twisted like the shell of a snail, then he imparted instructions to Sofie who passed them on to Linda. She was to stir the sand with her right forefinger, so bending down to him she did so, trying not to mind the smell of his robes which looked as if they hadn't been washed or even removed from the day he had put them on. She guessed that he probably slept in them and wiped his hands on them after eating his meals and performing other functions.

She was glad to straighten up and watch as he

166

peered at the sand pattern on the ground, then he began to rock back and forth, his eyes tightly closed for several seconds. In the silence Linda could hear the carpet merchants chanting the virtues of their wares and she heard lovely words like Tabriz and Bokhara, the places where the carpets had been woven.

Abruptly the diviner began to speak and Sofie listened to him intently while Perveneh clutched hold of Linda's arm and seemed a little frightened by the old man, whose lynx-like eyes were open again and fixed upon Linda.

In a while he paused and Linda wanted to know what he had said. 'Come on, Sofie, am I going to be happy or sad—or what?'

'He says——' Sofie looked a little lost. 'The sands tell him that you are going to make a journey across the desert and you will fly on wings, going very fast from a shadow that pursues you.'

Linda stared at Sofie and she felt her mouth go dry. 'Oh—it sounds like a lot of nonsense—ask him what he means.'

Sofie spoke to the diviner who shrugged and again peered at the sand pattern which looked meaningless to Linda. What journey would she possibly make with Karim away from her in Rabat? Even if she went riding in the desert she would obey his instructions and ride with Haid Saidi one of the household guards.

The diviner started muttering again and this time he added that the shadow couldn't help following her because it was in her heart and would journey with her.

'But where am I going?' she demanded.

'He says where the desert sands cannot reach.'

'Oh, it is a lot of rot and I should have listened to

you, Sofie. Here, give the old charlatan his money and let us go home to lunch—I'm ravenous!'

Back home at the *Ras Blanca* Linda ate a good lunch but she felt so lonely sitting alone in the *sala* with her coffee. The loneliness reminded her of her wedding day, when she had waited in here for Karim to come to her. She could see him now, so commanding and upright in his impeccable robes, his proud head bound with the ropes that made him look so utterly an Arab.

Curled among cushions she remembered how they had walked side by side along the colonnade . . . her heart had beat so fast with the many apprehensions of a bride. She had longed to be in his arms but she had been so afraid that he would find her wanting . . . a man of experience who had known lovely Arabian girls as well as European women of the world.

She sipped her coffee and every moment of her first intimate encounter with him was vibrantly memorable. Then a shadow crept into her eyes as she remembered the late-night scene which had followed their passionate hours of discovery in each others' arms. She didn't blame him for the bitterness of that scene, the harsh threat of rejection which, thank God, had resolved itself when he touched her again.

'We are never strangers when we touch,' he would say to her. But were they strangers when he was away from her and among those warlike men whose nature it was to hoard their grievances? They would talk about the political situation and the clashes with their enemy and Karim would be reminded of what Linda wanted him to forget.

Suddenly she needed the solace of her music and she went to the piano and opened it. She ran supple fingers along the keyboard and started to play the romantic music of George Gershwin, recalling those impromptu concerts at the college of music when the students would feel in the mood for some modern music.

Not that Gershwin would be considered modern any more but in Linda's opinion his music was close to being classical and she favoured in particular *The Man I Love*.

Though Linda had chosen to study the cello in particular she had a silken touch when it came to the piano and she remembered a fellow student saying to her that she would never need to starve; that if she failed to achieve her ambition to be a solo cellist she could make her living playing in one of those moody cocktail bars that catered for the kind of customer who wanted to indulge in nostalgia.

She wandered into *Rhapsody in Blue*, smiling to herself because when she played the rhapsody she always had a tendency to try and imitate the volatile style of Oscar Levant. She had possessed his recording until it had finally scratched itself to death because she played it so often.

At sunset she went riding with Haid Saidi, a lean Arab who spoke Spanish so she was able to converse with him. He was the same age as Karim; they had been in the army together and ever since he had been employed by the Sheikh and Linda was aware as they rode across the sands, aglow with the many colours that filled the sky when the sun died away, that he was studying her with his hawkish eyes in a face rather darker than Karim's because he had no dash of Latin blood.

'I heard you playing the piano, my lady,' he remarked. 'You have an excellent touch.'

'It's kind of you to say so.' Though she often saw

him tall and lean about the house, always clad in his Arab robes, she had not had occasion to hold a proper conversation with him. This evening she was glad of his company and the fact that Karim trusted him like a brother . . . this, after all, was the first night she would spend at the *Ras Blanca* without her husband.

'European music is so very different from the music of the East,' she remarked.

'The East and the West are worlds apart,' he replied.

'Then do you disapprove of me as the Sheikh's wife?' She eyed him curiously from beneath the brim of her hat, for tonight she had felt the need to be European and so she wore a dip-brim hat and a tweed jacket with her riding breeches and boots.

'It isn't my business to have an opinion, my lady, but as it so happens I consider you a very charming woman.'

Linda's pulses gave a jolt but she retained her air of composure; she didn't want Haid Saidi to guess that she suddenly felt less sure of him than when they had started their ride. How could she be sure of him when her own husband was an unknown quantity, much like the desert which to a newcomer like herself had no certain landmarks she could follow if she went astray.

'This morning in the bazaar I had my fortune told by one of those wizened old men who read the sand grains—are such men to be believed?' she asked.

'Who knows?' A cryptic smile edged his mouth. 'The hand of fate shuffles all of us like a pack of cards.'

'He said some strange things and I—I can't get them out of my mind.'

'The girl Perveneh related those strange things to me, my lady.'

'Oh?' Linda gave him a curious look. 'Do you ask her questions about me?'

'Arabs have enquiring minds.'

'So you encourage my personal maid to be—indiscreet?'

'Not really indiscreet, my lady.' His dark eyes glimmered into Linda's. 'She is a pretty creature who sometimes shares my company—ah, but don't be anxious, my lady, I would never lay a hand upon a young Arabian girl of virtue.'

'I should hope not!' Linda suddenly realised just how attractive Haid Saidi was, with not a spare inch of flesh on his strong facial bones. 'Perveneh is a nice girl and her marriage chances would be ruined if you——'

'She is a soft young dove and quite safe with me,' he murmured.

Linda couldn't help wondering if she, the Sheikh's wife, was altogether safe with this Arab who listened to her maid's innocent chatter and came to his own conclusions. In that instant she remembered what Karim had said, that it would be dangerous for her if his compatriots learned about her mother.

'You were in the army with Karim, weren't you?' she said, and her fingers had tightened on the reins of her horse.

'The Sheikh saved my life. We were searching a village for a pair of terrorists and I stepped inside a room where one of them held a pistol. He was about to pack me off to hell or heaven when El Khalid came flying through the back window like a winged hawk and he had a knife in his hand. A knife in the hand of an Arab is a swift and deadly weapon, my lady.'

Linda kept her features composed, for here in the desert where the stars were so numerous there was always a luminosity in the air and Haid Saidi had his eyes upon her face. 'I have noticed that everyone thinks of my husband as being purely Arabian, but he does have a Spanish side to him.'

'And which do you prefer, my lady?'

'I have no preference.'

'Have you not?'

'And you haven't any right to be so inquisitive.'

'Arabs are inquisitive and I am entirely of the East.'

'Do you basically disapprove of the Sheikh's choice of a wife?'

'My Lady Linda, a man takes for his wife the woman who pleases him best and it's apparent to us all that you have found great favour in his eyes. Among the Berbers he is a very popular man and he is with them in Rabat because they want him to take on the overall leadership, the position held by his father at the time he was assassinated. El Khalid has always divided his loyalties between Spain and the Berber regions but now he has married a wife in Fez there are hopes that he will remain here.'

Linda sat quiet in the saddle, staring ahead of her into the black and silver desert. 'Have you any idea what his decision will be?' she asked, and her earlier feeling of desolation had crept back into her heart.

'That decision, my lady, rests between him and Allah.'

'He loves his people, doesn't he?'

'Arabian loyalty has no peer.'

'And Karim would be so right for the job, wouldn't he?'

'Many think so.'

'I—I think so myself.' She suddenly urged her horse into a canter, then into a gallop, and the stars shimmered blindly in her tear-filled eyes. Karim's decision, as she knew, rested between him and a name carved into a little gold heart.

The following morning at the *Ras Blanca* the hand of fate dealt Linda a card with a sinister face on it. She went into Karim's dressing room in order to put away in his bureau the embossed belt which she had bought him in the bazaar. She didn't intend to pry but just needed some sensory contact with him by fingering his more intimate garments, especially a blue shirt which he had last worn on the journey from Spain.

As she lifted the shirt with the intention of pressing it to her face a buff envelope fell out as the shirt unfolded. It fell to the floor and Linda bent down to pick it up; her fingers felt something stiff and square inside and because the envelope was unsealed she took a look and discovered that the square object was a passport case in red calfskin, very similar to the one she had lost that first day in Spain when the cab which was taking her to Dona Domaya's house had driven into a sack of vegetables and spun half over the cliffside ... suspended there until Karim had arrived on the scene and taken charge.

Even as she withdrew the passport from the envelope Linda knew what she was going to find inside. There was her very own picture, her eyes wide and guileless, and there were the folded documents which according to Karim had gone missing in the sea when the cab had plunged down the cliffside.

He had sworn to her that her passport and papers were lost, yet here she stood with those same objects in her hand. He had actually used them to bring her into Fez Eldjid and she hadn't questioned him when he had said that he'd been able to acquire temporary documents that would permit her to enter the country.

Karim had lied to her. He had deliberately made her

feel beholden to him for the passport case contained the money she had taken with her to Spain. Looking her directly in the eyes he had said that she was without a penny to her name; that her work visa and her permission to reside in Spain were gone forever.

Anger swept over her and she bundled the blue shirt back into the drawer and slammed it shut, then leaving the master suite she hastened along the colonnade to her own room, the passport case and its contents clutched in her hand. Damn him, he had given her no chance to resist his half-threats and his pursuasions. He had taken brazen advantage of her naïvety; she had suited his purpose in every respect until he had seen the name of her mother carved upon the heart that was as hard as his own heart.

To her relief her room was empty and when she closed the door behind her, she slid the bolt with determined fingers. There was nothing to keep her at the *Ras Blanca*. Karim no longer wanted a child from her, and if he decided to stay in Fez as a political leader then he would hardly want for a wife a woman who would be a source of potential danger to his position among the Berbers.

She would take nothing with her but her handbag, otherwise members of the staff would be suspicious if they saw her leaving the house with a suitcase. She was entitled to take a drive if she wished and she would tell the driver that she wanted to do some shopping at the airport where the shops sold modern goods. Karim's only honest action as she saw it was to leave her money intact inside her passport; there was sufficient to get her home and that was why she had taken that amount to Spain, in case her job as a *compañera* turned out to be disappointing.

In a mood of cold calmness she changed out of her

dress into a cream-coloured suit and she tucked a sweater inside her handbag. When she landed in England she would feel the change in the climate; already she felt a sense of coldness deep inside her. She felt betrayed by Karim and by her own feelings. She had allowed him to become very precious to her and it hurt indescribably that all along she had been his dupe.

The shy and lonely English girl whose innocent body had appealed to his Eastern appetite. She was about to wrench from her wrist the wide gold bracelet that was worth a small fortune when she decided to keep it as payment for the pleasure she had given him. Of that she could be sure! No man could be truly deceiving when it came to what he achieved in a woman's arms and the one thing she was sure of was that Karim had enjoyed to the full the many hours they had spent in exploring the sensual side of their relationship.

She carefully combed her hair and because she looked rather bleak she applied some make-up. The mirror reflected the jade *feisha* in the vee of her voile blouse and quite deliberately she removed the Hand of Fatma which she was always going to wear. She dropped it into the little gold box with the note he had pinned to the pillow where his head had rested beside her own.

A hard tremor of pain ran all through her body. Countless times she had kissed his mouth not knowing that he had lied to her, uncaring of the anguish he caused her. He was an arrogant, ruthless man who had to have all his own way . . . well, he wouldn't have the pleasure of telling her that he was going to untie their marriage knot because there was no place for her at the side of a paramount leader.

He would return to the *Ras Blanca* to find her gone.

Nervous but determined Linda made her way to the garage where the chauffeur was cleaning the cars and told him to drive her to the airport. He looked astonished but she was the Sheikha and also an infidel and he didn't pretend to know the workings of a *roumia*'s mind. He put on his jacket and his cap and Linda climbed into the back of the big black car, glad that the windows were covered so she could sit in the dimness with her sense of desolation.

She was sorry not to be able to say goodbye to Sofie and Perveneh but the three of them had enjoyed themselves in the bazaar and she hoped they would remember her with friendship.

As the car drove out of the great courtyard she lifted the blind over the rear window and gazed back at the lovely white house until it went out of view. Her throat felt blocked with unshed tears and all the way to the airport she held her hand to her throat as if holding in the sobs that wanted to break loose. She hated Karim . . . she loved him. She wanted never to see his face again . . . she would never be able to forget his face.

'I shan't be long,' she told the driver, whose Spanish was less proficient than Haid Saidi's. 'I need things I must buy in the airport shops.'

'*Si, lellah.*' He settled back with his cap over his eyes as Linda walked into the airport and made her way to the counter where the flights to Europe were booked. She was praying that she would be lucky enough to acquire a cancellation and she stood there in a silent torment as the girl made her enquiries. A flight to Madrid was possible and from there she might get a seat on the late-afternoon flight to Heathrow Airport.

Linda snapped it up. She would be on her way and

that was all that counted. She just wanted to put as many miles as possible between herself and Karim el Khalid. Forever she told herself as she made her way with other passengers into the boarding lounge.

It was dark and rather cold when Linda emerged from Heathrow Airport but she wasn't too concerned for she knew where she was going. There was a small hotel in Chelsea that took music students and Linda had telephoned Mrs Palmer the proprietor, whose daughter Olive had studied music at the same time as Linda. They had been quite good friends and Mrs Palmer knew her.

Yes, she had said, she would be only too glad to let Linda have accommodation at the Palm Court.

Little specks of rain touched the windows of the black cab as it drove Linda in the direction of Chelsea. Under the jacket of her suit she now wore the sweater which she had brought with her; she was glad of it after several weeks in the warmth of Fez. She felt tired, still rather dispirited, but quite certain of what she was going to do. She was going to pawn the gold bracelet, for it wasn't truly hers to sell, and she would be able to pay for her hotel room while she looked for a job.

All she knew was music so she would look for a job such as Olive Palmer had once suggested, that of a pianist in a club. A job would make her independent and as time went by she might start to forget that she had been for a few magical weeks the wife of a Sheikh.

Karim, she decided, would divorce her. It was comparatively easy for an Arab; all he had to do was to declare in front of witnesses that he no longer wanted her for his wife and the deed was done. He would be rid of someone who could prove a potential embarrassment to him, and she would be rid of a man who hadn't lied when he had said that he had never known what it was to love.

Love? Linda stared from the window of the cab. It was a state of illusion, a spell that when it broke left a feeling of disenchantment that was barely endurable. But she would endure. She would make a new life for herself, untouched by Karim whom she would probably never see again.

He would hardly come looking for her though he would shrewdly guess that she had returned to England. If he came looking her aunt and uncle wouldn't be able to put him on her trail. Her aunt didn't know Olive Palmer, though Linda had a slight notion that Uncle Henry had met her at one of the college concerts. Anyway, he wouldn't be likely to remember that brief meeting; he had always been a little absent minded and wrapped up in his books and his recordings of Mozart and Brahms.

Linda looked a little sad. She was fond of her uncle but she couldn't face Aunt Doris and her recriminations. The very thought of having Karim thrown in her face as a man who had destroyed her life was more than Linda could bear. He hadn't destroyed her ... not quite.

She was warmly welcomed into the cosy environs of the Palm Court and merely explained that a job she had taken out East had gone all wrong and so she had hurriedly returned to England in the hope of finding work in the capital. She was given cups of tea and ham sandwiches and was then allowed to go to bed. She crawled wearily beneath the covers and tired as she felt, lay shivering in the grip of a nervous reaction.

Everything had happened so swiftly ... instead of being in bed in a luxurious oriental room she lay in one of the more modest rooms of a small hotel in London. Instead of silk sheets she now lay between stiffly laundered cotton ones, and instead of hearing the cicadas in the starlit trees she heard the sound of a tug wailing its horn as it proceeded along the Thames. It was September and there was probably a mist on the river, and with this thought in mind Linda drifted off to sleep, worn out by her flight from Fez.

In the next few days Linda went job hunting with a vengeance; a job as a pianist seemed as if it would never materialise, and then she had a stroke of luck. The *Chez Lille* in Bruton Street placed an advertisement in the *Evening Standard*; they required someone to play the piano in the supper room and Linda telephoned at once for an appointment.

As it happened she was a member of the musicians' union, for like other music students she had hoped to perform in an earning capacity. Her change of heart and mind prior to her trip to Spain had been complex, tied up with impulses she had only partly understood at the time, but thankfully that union membership made it possible for the manager of *Chez Lille* to accept her as their supper room entertainer.

Linda was thrilled. She and Olive went shopping and she bought herself a simple but stylish evening dress in a subtle shade of apricot. It suited her bright hair and her tanned skin and she started her new career with enthusiasm. She played well and she loved to play and her repertoire ranged from classical pieces to the Gershwin music she had played that day when the sand diviner had seen her in flight, running to where the desert sands didn't reach.

It was a close friend of Olive's who brought her the piece of music that within a few months was to become her theme. From the intimate supper room of *Chez Lille* Linda went on to become the pianist in the Harmony Room of the Clarence Hotel, and the *Firebird* music initiated the dress of fire-coloured chiffon which she wore in the second half of her performance, when as the lights dimmed leaving only a tinted spotlight around her slim figure at the black grand piano a quietness fell over the diners and they watched entranced as Linda's slender fingers beat out a rhythm that was both sensuous and elusive . . . like love on the run, as a male customer had remarked to the elusive Linda Layne who only smiled her slightly sad smile whenever a man tried to become more than an admirer of her musical skills.

It got around among the stylish patrons of London night life that there was someone special to watch and listen to in the Harmony Room of the Clarence, as long established as the Ritz and equally handsome in its décor.

When Linda played the *Firebird* the cabaret audience were led to the brink of believing that tiny scarlet flames were leaping around her slim figure, an effect produced by a clever spotlight, the dress she wore and above all her playing. Always at the finale of the music the audience applauded madly and young men sometimes dashed after Linda as she slipped between the curtains, as if intent on beating out the flames that in their aroused imaginations were scorching her creamy skin.

When she entered her dressing-room Maudie quickly enclosed her in a wrap, for such intense playing made her feel as warm as if she had escaped from the flames of the music.

'So you still know the art of setting a man on fire.'

The deep timbre of the voice made Linda's heart

twist inside her. 'Oh, Maudie, why did you let him in?' It was a cry from the heart of her.

'Your dresser wisely knows that she couldn't keep me out,' he said. 'She also realises that you and I must speak privately together.'

'No——' Linda flung a look of desperation at the good-natured Cockney woman who had been her dresser ever since the start of her success. 'Please stay, Maudie!'

But Maudie was already opening the door. 'No, love, I'll make myself scarce for a while—as the gentleman says you have private things to discuss.'

The door closed behind her and Linda found herself alone with El Khalid for the first time in months. He still had a commanding air of distinction and authority, and he could still make her feel weak at the knees.

'Why have you come here?' Try as she might Linda couldn't keep a tremor out of her voice. 'W-what do you want?'

He studied the way her fingers plucked at the sash of her wrap, then slowly he lifted his gaze until it dwelt full on her face. 'Perhaps I came to hear you play.'

She flung the smoky-gold hair back from her brow. 'Do you consider that I've improved since those evenings when I used to play in the *sala* of your house?'

A furrow appeared between his black brows. 'It seems too long ago.' He took from his coat pocket the cigar case stamped with his initials.

'May I?' He drew open the case and there in a soldierly row were the brown, slim cigars that were specially blended for him. They always looked lethal but their aroma was sultry as a desert night.

'By all means.' She turned to the dressing-table and a glance in the mirror, lit by a glowing crescent of bulbs, showed her the lingering look of shock in her eyes. She had thought of Karim as being out of her life for always.

The remembered smoke of his cigar drifted to her, bringing with it potent memories of the desert when the sun started to cool and the sands beyond the white walls of *Ras Blanca* became an undulating carpet of many colours. The memories littered her thoughts as the stars in the desert sky, and silence lay between herself and Karim like a barrier, a silence underlined by the soft humming of the electric heater attached to the wall.

'By Allah, this country of yours is still a devilish cold place. As I stepped from the aircraft at Heathrow it was like landing in the Arctic.'

'Christmas is almost upon us.' Linda dared to look at Karim's reflection in the mirror and his eyes were penetrating her like knives that wanted to rip the silk and chiffon from her body. Those eyes swept up and down her figure as if he were looking for some alteration in her looks.

'Why did you run away from me?' he demanded, so suddenly that he made her almost jump out of her skin.

'Y-you know why.'

'I knew when I returned from Rabat what motivated you, you had found your passport and papers, but I never really knew why you left me.'

Linda turned from the mirror and beneath the smoky-gold, tumbling hair her tawny eyes were tormented. 'Is it so strange,' she asked, 'that a wife should leave a husband who never loved her?'

He gazed fiercely into her face, which was suddenly

all bleakness and fine bone. His eyes raked her plume of hair, her creamy skin, her mouth that was poignant with the pain that had never really gone away. Only when she played her music did she forget him, but now he stood before her and she wanted to hate him for making her love him all over again.

'Does it seem strange to you,' he asked, 'that I have never stopped looking for you? Your relatives had no notion of where you were and it was only by chance that in the bar of the Dorchester I heard someone mention your name and I then discovered that you were playing the piano here at the Clarence.'

Linda tilted her chin and gathered her pride together. 'Why come looking for me, Karim? I thought I did you a good turn by running away from you—I knew that when you returned from Rabat you would tell me that our marriage was over.'

'Over?' His eyes drilled into her. 'I don't follow you.'

'How could you be supreme leader of your tribe and have me for a wife?' She raised her wrist on which swung the little gold heart. 'I am Miriam's daughter, am I not?'

'And you are also the wife of El Khalid.' He tossed the cigar into the wash-basin where it spat sparks as he came and relentlessly gathered Linda into his arms. 'Did you ever really believe that I would surrender you for the sake of putting more ropes of office around my headcloth? Do I look a fool?'

He took her chin in his hand and raised her face to his and never had she seen his eyes so burningly black, so fiercely insistent, so devouring.

'The only foolish thing I ever did where you are concerned was to say that I couldn't feel love. I haven't stopped feeling it since the day we met. I haven't had a night of peace since I returned from Rabat and you weren't at *Ras Blanca* to run into my arms. My arms have only just stopped aching for you. I love and cherish you till I die. If you require, my very dearest Linda, then I shall shout it from the rooftops of London as the *muezzin* shouts the prayer from the minarets. I adore you—want you—and, by Allah, I won't be denied. I won't be, do you hear me?'

Linda gazed up at him, as helpless as she had been that first day in his limousine when he held her for the first time in his arms and they forgot to be strangers when they touched.

'But—I have my career——'

'To hell with your career!'

'You—you told me a pack of lies——'

'So I did.' He quite shamelessly smiled. 'I'd have told several packets of them just to get my hands on you.'

'You truly are the most arrogant man in the world.'

'And you,' almost gently he stroked her hair, 'you are divine.'

'Oh, Karim——' She could feel herself melting into him ... all her brave resolve was ebbing away. 'Karim——'

'Yes, my dear heart?'

'Did you really go and see my Aunt Doris and Uncle Henry?'

'Of course I did. I acquired the address in Essex from my cousin Ramos and went to see them as swiftly as possible. They could tell me nothing and were extremely anxious about you. On that first visit to England I did my utmost to find you, then I returned to Spain in the hope that you had gone looking for another job as a *compañera*. Nothing! *Nada!*'

He gazed down at her and he held her bruisingly

close as if even yet he couldn't quite believe that they were together again, that they were touching and the search for her was over. 'You have put me through hell, do you realise it, *bint*?'

She nodded, for now they were close like this she could see that his face was fine-drawn as if anxiety had eaten away at him. She slowly raised a hand and touched his face. 'I didn't think you really wanted me, Karim——'

'By Allah, how can you say such a thing?' He gave her a punishing shake. 'I thought all sorts of things— that you had been kidnapped and taken to some house of infamy. Haid Saidi and I left no stone unturned and then I decided to come to England again in the hope that you had visited your relatives. Tell me why you stayed away from them?'

'Because I—I wanted to be anonymous.'

'And luckily for me achieved it,' he said sarcastically, 'by becoming a nightclub celebrity. What am I to do with such a girl?'

'Do you truly love me, Karim?'

'Are you not woman enough to know that I love you?' he mocked. 'Think, my *bint*. Think of the night before I left for Rabat. In the morning I left you with great reluctance but I had to confront the Sheikhs in order to tell them my reasons for refusing the honour they wished to bestow on me. It was courtesy that I tell them to their faces, but the days dragged and the nights were without end—you will never know my torture when I arrived home and you were gone.'

A look of torture was there in his eyes when he said: 'It was as if a sabre had slashed me in half ... you were gone from my side and where you had been there was an aching emptiness. Well, you sorely punished me for the deception I played on you, Linda, and I should have remembered that wives go looking in pockets and drawers when a husband is away on business.'

'Oh, I was being sentimental, Karim, I wanted to touch something personal of yours and out fell my passport.'

'I see.' His features softened. 'You wanted to feel in contact with me?'

'Yes.'

'Then if I forgive you, *adorada*, will you forgive me?'

'Oh yes!'

'Never, never strangers when we touch, my darling girl.'

'Never, never lonely when we kiss, my darling Karim.'

They were still kissing when Maudie poked an enquiring head around the door . . . so that was who he was, he was Miss Linda's gentleman.

Coming Next Month in Harlequin Presents!

855   A FOREVER AFFAIR   Rosemary Carter
Despite its savage beauty, her husband's African game reserve is
no longer home. Was it carved in stone that she could never love
another man? Surely a divorce would change that!

856   PROMISE OF THE UNICORN   Sara Craven
To collect on a promise, a young woman returns her talisman—
the protector of virgins—to its original owner. The power of the
little glass unicorn was now with him!

857   AN IRRESISTIBLE FORCE   Ann Charlton
A young woman is in danger of being taken over by a subtle
irresistible force rather than by open aggression when she takes
on an Australian construction king who's trying to buy out her
grandmother.

858   INNOCENT PAWN   Catherine George
Instead of looking past the money to the man behind it, a mother
is prompted by panic to blame her husband when their five-year-
old daughter is kidnapped.

859   MALIBU MUSIC   Rosemary Hammond
California sunshine and her sister's beach house provide the
atmosphere a young woman needs to focus on her future—until
her neighbor tries to seduce her.

860   LADY SURRENDER   Carole Mortimer
The man who bursts into her apartment can't see why his best
friend would throw away his marriage for a woman like her. But
soon he can't imagine any man—married or otherwise—*not*
falling for her.

861   A MODEL OF DECEPTION   Margaret Pargeter
A model takes on an assignment she can't handle when she tries
to entice a man into selling his island in the Caribbean. She was
supposed to deceive the man, not fall in love.

862   THE HAWK OF VENICE   Sally Wentworth
Most people travel to Venice to fall in love. Instead, an au pair girl
makes the journey to accuse a respected Venetian count of
kidnapping—or of seduction, at least.

Here's how to get this special offer from Harlequin! As simple as 1...2...3!

SEPTEMBER
TREASURY EDITION
COUPON

1. Each month, save one Treasury Edition coupon from your favorite Romance or Presents novel.
2. In four months you'll have saved four Treasury Edition coupons (<u>only</u> one coupon per month allowed).
3. Then all you have to do is fill out and return the order form provided, along with the four Treasury Edition coupons required and $1.00 for postage and handling.

Mail to: Harlequin Reader Service

RT1-B-2

In the U.S.A.
2504 West Southern Ave.
Tempe, AZ 85282

In Canada
P.O. Box 2800, Postal Station A
5170 Yonge Street
Willowdale, Ont. M2N 6J3

Please send me my FREE copy of the Janet Dailey Treasury Edition. I have enclosed the four Treasury Edition coupons required and $1.00 for postage and handling along with this order form.

(Please Print)

NAME_____

ADDRESS_____

CITY_____

STATE/PROV._____ ZIP/POSTAL CODE_____

SIGNATURE_____

This offer is limited to one order per household.

SUPPLIES LIMITED

This special Janet Dailey offer expires January 1986.

EYE OF THE STORM

MAURA SEGER

A powerful portrayal of the events of World War II in the Pacific, *Eye of the Storm* is a riveting story of how love triumphs over hatred. In this, the first of a three-book chronicle, Army nurse Maggie Lawrence meets Marine Sgt. Anthony Gargano. Despite military regulations against fraternization, they resolve to face together whatever lies ahead.... Author Maura Seger, also known to her fans as Laurel Winslow, Sara Jennings, Anne MacNeil and Jenny Bates, was named 1984's Most Versatile Romance Author by *The Romantic Times*.

Take 4 novels and a surprise gift FREE

Six exciting series for you every month... from Harlequin

Harlequin Romance·
The series that started it all

Tender, captivating and heartwarming...
love stories that sweep you off to faraway places
and delight you with the magic of love.

◆

Harlequin Presents·
Powerful contemporary love stories...as individual as the women who read them

The No. 1 romance series...
exciting love stories for you, the woman of today...
a rare blend of passion and dramatic realism.

◆

Harlequin Superromance®
It's more than romance...
it's Harlequin Superromance

A sophisticated, contemporary romance-fiction
series, providing you with a longer,
more involving read...a richer mix of complex plots,
realism and adventure.

Harlequin
American Romance™
Harlequin celebrates the American woman...

...by offering you romance stories written about American women, by American women for American women. This series offers you contemporary romances uniquely North American in flavor and appeal.

◆

Harlequin Temptation T.M.
Passionate stories for today's woman

An exciting series of sensual, mature stories of love...dilemmas, choices, resolutions... all contemporary issues dealt with in a true-to-life fashion by some of your favorite authors.

◆

Harlequin Intrigue™
Because romance can be quite an adventure

Harlequin Intrigue, an innovative series that blends the romance you expect... with the unexpected. Each story has an added element of intrigue that provides a new twist to the Harlequin tradition of romance excellence.

Harlequin Books

PROD-A-2